Make a Joyful Noise

JENNY WORSTALL

ISBN-10: 1478325542
ISBN-13: 978-1478325543

For Norman, David and Penny,

with love.

CONTENTS

Chapter One: Sing aloud

"Slain!"

"No, no, no - you make it sound about as interesting as a tea party at the Women's Institute. Belshazzar has been slain by an unknown hand after a riotous evening of blasphemy and feasting with his concubines. Can't you use your imaginations?"

The sopranos and altos gazed at their conductor with adoration; they would try to do anything he asked, anything at all. Just then Tristan dropped his pencil. Five altos and two tenors jostled one another to retrieve it; the lucky alto who won was rewarded with a dazzling smile and the promise of a drink in the pub later. Lucy gave a sigh and shifted in her chair. Tristan glanced in her direction and exclaimed,

"Now come on ladies and gentlemen - we must get to the end of this section before the break. Imagine the scene of gross over indulgence and pleasure before the horrific night when the king meets his grisly end... try to aim the voices high for maximum effect when you shout "Slain!" It is a shout full of passion and bloodcurdling harshness."

Lucy put her entire self, body and soul, into the next "Slain!" After all, Tristan had personally asked her to.

"A little better, ladies and gentlemen," said Tristan despondently. "But you will have to try harder when we rehearse with the orchestra and soloists later on. It just isn't exciting enough yet."

Lucy felt a sense of failure wash over her as Tristan continued, rather tiredly,

"Well, perhaps we will try again after the break. You all seem very flat this evening."

Several leading sopranos looked up indignantly, wounded by this insult, but their chorus master was oblivious to their feelings and continued,

"We all need a break - God knows I do anyway - so let's try again after coffee."

During the break, Lucy found herself standing next to a rather shy young man called Steve. He had been trying to introduce himself to her for several weeks now and had begun to despair of ever having an opportunity to do so. Lucy gave him her attention for a few minutes while he told her that he was a teacher at one of the local secondary schools, but she soon lost interest. She spent all day surrounded by teachers and had joined the choral society to meet more exciting people.

Lucy looked around to try to see where Tristan was. He was so wild and passionate looking, she thought, rather like Heathcliff, although she doubted whether Heathcliff would have raised his little finger when drinking coffee in quite the same way as Tristan. Would Heathcliff have drunk coffee at all, Lucy wondered. Perhaps a flagon of rough ale would have been his preferred choice?

Lucy wanted to go over to Tristan and join the band of admirers clustered around him. If only she had the courage! A soprano was eagerly persuading Tristan to consume vast quantities of custard creams; she was shaking her magnificent glossy hair as she actually held a biscuit up to Tristan's lips for him to nibble. How obvious can you get, thought Lucy in disgust. Miss Custard Cream, you should be ashamed of yourself! I should think that Tristan is very embarrassed by that sort of behaviour. Just then, to Lucy's surprise, Tristan put his arm round the soprano's waist, presumably to gently push her away Lucy thought, but the soprano must have misunderstood and put her head on his shoulder. Lucy could hear raucous laughter from some of the basses and then Tristan hastily clapped his hands and called for the chorus to reassemble.

Lucy made her way back to her place without noticing that Steve was trying to catch her eye. Her thoughts drifted away as the rehearsal continued. She imagined Tristan putting his hand round her waist, Tristan murmuring sweet nothings in her ear, even Tristan kissing her… Lucy came back to earth with a jolt as the pianist thumped out some fortissimo chords. The rehearsal pianist, Miss Greymitt, was long past her prime and what with her arthritic fingers and slight deafness was often the target of Tristan's scorn.

"No, no, no," shouted Tristan, "that won't do at all. Go from the top of the page."

He stood alert, hands outstretched, as the singers found the right place. All except for Andy in the basses, who was reading the Financial Times and of course the back row of sopranos who were still chatting animatedly about their antics in "The Blue Orchid" night club the previous evening. Tristan waited for their chatter to subside, then gave Miss Greymitt a murderous look; she was peering at her music anxiously, searching in vain for the right place to start.

"In your own time, Miss Greymitt," Tristan said sarcastically.

"Oh dear, I mean, oh, which bar is it, Mr Proudfoot, I mean, Tristan? You see, my edition has different page numbers, wouldn't you know, such a nuisance, so sorry…"

Miss Greymitt's voice trailed off as she looked round at the front row of singers for support but they were all gazing at Tristan with rapt attention, cheeks flushed and mouths open, ready to take a breath whenever he gave them the upbeat.

"Two bars after figure 32," bellowed Tristan. "Give the choir their notes please."

Miss Greymitt's eyes misted over and she gave the altos an E flat instead of an E.

"If you want something done, do it yourself," grumbled Tristan under his breath.

"May I?" he asked with exaggerated politeness as he stretched over Miss Greymitt's arms, which were encased in olive green tweed as usual.

I bet she's worn that suit for the last thirty years, thought Lucy in amazement and I bet she calls it a "costume". Tristan stabbed at the correct notes, leapt back onto the podium and they were off.

"Praise ye," rang out the sopranos and altos.

"Praise ye the god of brass," barked the men.

Miss Greymitt nearly gave up completely at this point as the accompaniment became ever more fiendish - it was a notorious black spot for rehearsal pianists - but somehow she managed to keep some sort of accompaniment going with her left hand, just to give an idea of the rhythm. Tristan rolled his eyes but did not offer to take over again at the keyboard. Even he knew his pianistic talent had its limitations.

Steve moved his chair slightly so that he could look along the row of singers to Lucy. He noticed that she was frowning slightly and looked rather nervous. What's worrying her, he wondered. I hope she's all right.

Lucy was thinking of tomorrow's teaching. This was her first job and she was finding it quite a baptism of fire. Still, at least these weekly choir practices gave her something to look forward to and it would be the concert in a few weeks time. Perhaps Tristan would have noticed her by then?

At the end of the rehearsal Lucy looked around, hoping that someone she knew would be going to the pub and that she could tag along. She knew that the main social life of the choir went on in the pub and she desperately wanted to join in. Tristan and his entourage made a noisy exit and was it Lucy's imagination or did Tristan glance in her direction with a smile as he tossed his red cashmere scarf over one shoulder on his way out?

Lucy said rather desperately to her friend Sarah sitting next to her,

"I don't suppose you fancy going to the pub, do you?"

"Well why not?" answered Sarah. "I mean to say, we have to have a social life, don't we, especially after the grilling Tristan's given us."

Sarah led the way out of the hall and Lucy followed sheepishly.

"You're not getting keen on Tristan, are you?"

interrogated Sarah as they hurried along the damp streets to the pub. "You know he's been married twice, don't you and he's got a terrible reputation."

"That doesn't bother me," answered Lucy. "It just means he's had a tough time. Not that I'm interested at all, of course," she added quickly. "How are your family, anyway?"

"Oh, fine I suppose," said Sarah, "although little James did have a nasty cough last week. . ."

Sarah was a friend of Lucy's older sister, Caroline. When Lucy had moved to Springfield for her first teaching job, Caroline had put the two of them in contact with each other and Sarah had encouraged Lucy to join the choir.

"A great way to meet people, you know," Sarah had explained to Lucy. "They're all very friendly - lots of nice young men too - you'll soon find your feet. Sit next to me for the first few sessions if you like. It'll make things easier."

And so Lucy had joined the choir and had sat next to Sarah, enduring her slightly flat, raucous singing with tolerance.

She means well, thought Lucy, but I wish she'd listen to what Tristan says. Once she's made a mistake, she repeats it every time and she's so out of tune - still, without her, I suppose I wouldn't have joined the choir and I really am grateful for that.

They had nearly reached the pub doors when it began to rain heavily. Lucy quickly pulled her hood over her head. It wouldn't do for Tristan to see her with panda eyes and frizzy hair.

"We're nearly there," shouted Sarah with a burst of laughter. "I don't bother about the rain. It's the only beauty treatment I get!"

She tossed her head back and let the rain cascade over her face. She didn't have to worry about panda eyes because she wasn't wearing any make up.

Not even a dab of lipstick, thought Lucy in

amazement. The rain ran through Sarah's wiry hair and squeezed it into little curls.

"Once you've got two kids, you don't have time for anything," laughed Sarah. "The world will just have to take me as it finds me. Now, you mustn't let me stay long because Brian will expect me back by ten o'clock. I shouldn't really be here at all, but I want to make sure you're all right."

"Thank you," said Lucy humbly. "You've been so kind to me, helping me to settle in and make friends."

"Nonsense," said Sarah, "it's been a pleasure. You must come and have lunch with us soon. What about this Sunday? I could get Caroline and family to come too; you know they're up in London for the weekend, don't you? There's some computer fair or something that Jeremy's going to at Earl's Court on the Saturday, so they're making a weekend of it, staying with Jeremy's brother in Putney. I don't see enough of Caroline since they moved down to Bath, but I know they're really happy down there; after all, you and Caroline grew up there, didn't you? And of course most of Jeremy's work is in Bristol now, not London and the schools are better down there, or so Caroline says. Now Lucy, I'm sure you don't eat properly in that flat of yours. Look at you! You're all skin and bone! Come and have some decent home cooking. Are you free this Sunday?"

They were in the pub by now.

"Great," said Lucy, although her heart sank a little at the thought of seeing her sister, Caroline. "Yes, I'm free and I'd love to come to lunch."

Suddenly Lucy spotted Tristan at the bar.

"Let me get you a drink," Lucy said eagerly to Sarah. "No, I insist. You wait here and I'll be back in a minute."

Lucy ran her hands through her hair and pulled her stomach in as she approached the bar. Tristan turned to look at her with his lazy charming smile. Lucy thought she would be sick with nerves.

"Can I get you a drink?" he asked softly. His eyes closed slightly and he held out his hand to her. "We haven't been properly introduced, have we? I've noticed you in the sopranos for a few weeks now and of course I remember you from your audition. Lavinia, isn't it? Or Lucy? Yes, Lucy, Well, hello Lucy. How do you like my choir? What made you join?"

"Well," stammered Lucy, frantically trying to pull her hand away from Tristan's firm, warm grasp. "My friend Sarah, she's over there, that is, she thought I could meet people, I mean, I like singing, no, I love singing and I was in the choir at school and college and now I'm teaching and …"

"Well, I'm sure we're lucky to have you," drawled Tristan. "Now, about that drink."

Just then, the girl who had fed Tristan the custard cream came over and Lucy muttered that she had better get back to her friend Sarah.

"Another time," said Tristan as he was led away. "Definitely another time. I look forward to it."

Miss Custard Cream glared angrily at Lucy from the other side of the pub but Lucy was totally oblivious.

I've talked to Tristan, she thought with joy. He wants to see me again. If only I hadn't been with Sarah, I could be having a drink with him right now. Oh, how handsome he is! And his voice is so low and smooth and, well, sexy I suppose. I can't wait for next week. I'll just turn round now and see if I can see him.

"What took you so long?" laughed Sarah when Lucy brought her drink over. "Now don't tell me you're falling for that old charmer, Tristan. He's not suitable for permanent attachment you know."

"I can talk to him, can't I?" said Lucy sharply, then, slightly ashamed of herself, she added, "Oh, I'm sorry Sarah, it's just that to be honest I do think he's rather gorgeous but obviously nothing's going to happen between us, is it? I mean he wouldn't be interested in me, would he?"

"You'd be surprised," said Sarah grimly as she looked at Lucy, noticing her creamy white skin and abundant red wavy hair with a worried frown. "How about your work?" she asked. "What are the other staff like? Any potential suitors there?"

"Oh, I don't know," said Lucy. "I always seem to be so busy and I'm keen to get my classes under control while I'm still new, so I don't tend to socialise with the other staff much, except for Julia of course, because I'm sharing her flat."

"That's a pity," mused Sarah. "Well, you could do worse than look at the men in the choir, you know; what about that young man I saw you with in the break?"

"Yes, Steve I think his name was," said Lucy. "Yes, he seems nice but…"

Lucy broke off and turned to look wistfully in Tristan's direction. Just then, he gazed across at her and actually winked. Lucy blushed with pleasure.

I can see that I'm going to have to have a word with Lucy's sister, Caroline, thought Sarah protectively. I can't watch a lamb going to the slaughter, certainly not such a loveable lamb as Lucy. It isn't right. And yet Sarah had to admit to herself that when she had first joined the choir all those years ago when she was single, Tristan had certainly caused her heart to beat faster, but of course he hadn't given her a second glance. Whereas Lucy, now Lucy was different, she was just the sort of girl that Tristan might want to fall for. Yes, thought Sarah. I'll give Caroline a ring tomorrow and mention this little situation. I'm sure I wouldn't be interfering, it's just that once you're a mother, you know how to look after people and I couldn't bear to see Lucy made unhappy. After all, her own mother is so far away, in France.

"Oh my goodness!" said Sarah to Lucy suddenly, coming out of her daydream with a jolt. "Is that the time? My darling husband will be pretty fed up if I don't make a move for home now. Would you like a lift, Lucy? No? Well, be careful on the bus, won't you?"

With a short bark of laughter, Sarah fastened up her bright red puffa jacket and was gone, reappearing a couple of seconds later to ask,

"You'll be all right then? And we look forward to seeing you on Sunday!"

Lucy nodded and smiled and Sarah was finally gone. Lucy noticed with annoyance that Tristan was also leaving, with Miss Custard Cream on his arm. Oh well, Lucy thought, I suppose I may as well get going. After all, I've got a few lessons to prepare for tomorrow, although I sometimes wonder what the point is. I don't know what I could possibly do to prepare myself for a music lesson with Year 9. Take a karate course possibly, or transform myself into an incredibly frightening and powerful monster. Just developing the capacity to shout loudly enough so that they could hear me over the chaos would be a start, I suppose.

Lucy stood up to go and then heard a voice.

"Oh, hello Lucy! How are you?"

Lucy turned to see Deborah, the choir secretary, bearing down on her.

"Just checking up to see if you can make the orchestral rehearsal in December. It's on the afternoon on the 14th of December, the day of the concert."

"Yes, I know," answered Lucy. "I'll be there."

"And can I give you some tickets to sell for the concert? You might have to push them a bit because Walton isn't everyone's cup of tea, especially near Christmas, in fact I think Tristan had taken leave of his senses when he planned the music for this concert, but there you are, he's the boss! And there is that lovely Vivaldi Concerto in the first half of the concert, so maybe people will come to hear that."

Deborah stood squarely in front of Lucy, observing her with eager interest while some other choir members were trying in vain to squeeze past her.

"Oh dearie me!" bellowed Deborah. "I'm in the way again! Time I started that diet I suppose! Well you're skinny enough Lucy, I must say. Looks like you could do with a bit more meat on your bones. It's not healthy to be too thin, you know!"

"So people often tell me," remarked Lucy with a half smile. "It's not something I seem to have much control over. Thanks for the tickets - I'll do my best to sell them."

"Good egg!" shouted Deborah. "So glad you've settled in. See you next week at the rehearsal!"

Lucy made a quick escape and ran through the puddles to the bus stop.

When she arrived home, she found her flatmate Julia lying full length on the sofa watching "Who wants to be a millionaire."

Take this box of chocolates away from me, won't you Lucy?" Julia begged. "I've eaten at least half of them and I shall be as fat as a pig, no, fatter than a pig, if I go on like this. . . no, wait, I'll just have another and that's my favourite, oh, it's no good, I just can't help it. Have one yourself. Please, eat them all!"

Lucy took one and nibbled the corner but it tasted sickly sweet and she threw it in the bin.

"Will you come to our concert Julia?" Lucy asked. "I've got some tickets to sell and it won't be too bad I think. The choir is definitely improving."

"It's not really my scene," said Julia, looking worried. "I'm not sure I know how to behave at a classical concert. Besides, I might get the giggles when I see this conductor bloke you're always going on about, old Tristan whatever he's called."

"Tristan Proudfoot," retorted Lucy primly.

"What a name!" shrieked Julia and then Lucy began to giggle too. "Come on," continued Julia, "let me make you a cup of tea and we can get down to some serious gossip."

"Actually," said Lucy, "I've got a bit of a headache

coming on so I think I'll have a bath and go straight to bed. Anyway, we're teaching tomorrow; it's not the weekend yet."

"I know," answered Julia, "but I've only got sixth formers all morning, so I'm not worried."

"Lucky you," said Lucy sadly. "I seem to have all the worst classes. I don't think I'll be allowed to teach the GCSE and A'level classes for a year or so," she continued, "that is, if I'm still there by then."

"It can't be that bad," laughed Julia. "Oh crikey, don't cry Lucy, I mean, is it that bad? I had no idea."

"I'm just tired," sobbed Lucy. "It will seem OK in the morning I expect."

Julia put her arm round Lucy.

"The first year of teaching is always difficult and some of our kids can be absolute buggers, I admit, but Luce, you've got to talk to your head of department. I'm sure she'll help you. What about it? Do you want me to say anything?"

"Oh no" said Lucy hastily. "It's all right, really it is! I'm just tired and I'll be fine in the morning. Good night Julia, good night."

But Lucy shed a few more tears in the bath and it wasn't until she was asleep in bed and had begun to dream about Tristan that her face softened and the frown between her eyes finally relaxed. She imagined that Tristan was putting his arm round her waist and whispering to her. His face came close and she could feel his breath on her neck as he held her gently.

"Oh Tristan," gasped Lucy. Tristan didn't say anything, but moved closer to her. Lucy smiled and stirred slightly in her sleep. She stretched out her hands and pulled her battered old teddy towards her, the teddy she had loved since childhood, the teddy with one eye missing and with a split down the side where the stuffing was leaking out.

"Oh Tristan," Lucy whispered to her teddy, "Oh

Tristan, my darling."

Teddy gazed impassively at the ceiling with his one eye. He was not unlike Tristan in many ways; a little tubby round the middle, a little threadbare on top, maybe a little past his prime but with an irresistible charm that made Lucy love him. She was choosing the colour of her bridesmaids' dresses by now and wondering whether Tristan would think Widor's "Toccata" was a little too popular and obvious to walk down the aisle to. Perhaps a less well known French organ symphony would be a much more interesting and unusual choice, she pondered. But no, Lucy was set on Widor's "Toccata" and the Tristan in her dreams murmured,

"Of course you must have the music you love, my darling; after all, this is the most important day of our lives and I want you to be happy with every detail."

Lucy frowned slightly. Even she was finding it hard to reconcile this dream Tristan with the rather egocentric and impatient musician she knew him to be. No, she would let Tristan choose all the music; whatever he wanted would be what she wanted because she knew they thought alike on all the important things. Although I do think he is rather unkind to Miss Greymitt, thought Lucy disloyally, but then a man of such genius would obviously find it hard to tolerate incompetence.

The dream Tristan took Lucy in his arms again and Lucy smiled and surrendered herself to a deep untroubled sleep.

Chapter Two: A great feast

"Get out of my way!"

"No, you move! I was here first!"

Two diminutive creatures were fighting with plastic swords and shields on the stairs.

"Be careful you two," begged their mother, Sarah, as she squeezed past them with an armful of washing.

"You know we've got guests arriving in a few minutes, don't you and there's so much to get ready. Why don't you go and lay the table with Daddy?"

"No fear," replied James. "We're not doing that! We're too busy fighting. This is my castle, Thomas, so take that! And that!"

Sarah shook her head then rushed off to the kitchen.

"Washing, trifle, turn the roast potatoes over. . . Oh! I haven't even put the potatoes in yet!"

She stared at the tray of white fluffy potatoes in oil with dismay. She had done everything correctly, had boiled the potatoes for ten minutes, then bashed them about in the saucepan to fluff up the edges so that they would be extra crispy, then put them in hot oil, all just as Delia Smith had commanded. But then she had forgotten to put the tray in the oven!

"Oh no," screamed Sarah. "What shall I do?"

Her husband, alerted by her cries and fearing some sort of major accident requiring a trip to casualty, rushed into the room.

"What's happened?" he demanded. "What's the problem? Oh I see," he added more gently, as he saw his wife crumpled in a chair, pointing mutely at the potatoes. "Forgotten to put them in, have you? Don't worry darling."

Brian had been married to Sarah for nearly ten years, but was still surprised by the depth of her feelings when faced with what he considered a trivial problem, just as he was amazed by her fortitude in times of real trouble. With one stride he was at his wife's side to give her a hug, then he slid the dish of potatoes into the oven.

"Lucky you remembered to put the oven on," Brian smiled. "They'll be done in no time and anyway Caroline's always late. It's going to be a lovely meal. You've done really well."

Sarah smiled gratefully at her husband. Just then, James ran into the kitchen.

"Mummy! Thomas won't let me stab him!"

"Good for Thomas," remarked Sarah as she got to her feet. "I'm glad one of you has got some sense."

She ruffled James' hair as he stood in front of her and planted a quick kiss on his forehead.

"Now, run along darling, our guests will be here any minute. By the way, where is Thomas?"

James raised his eyebrows and laughed, hopping from one foot to the other.

"Oh no," said Sarah crossly. "You haven't shut him in the study again, have you? You know he can't manage the door handle."

Listening intently, she could just make out the muffled screams of her younger son.

"Go and let him out - no, on second thoughts I'll go."

Sarah bounded up the stairs and as she opened the study door carefully, an enraged toddler shot out, bellowing at the top of his voice,

"I want my mummy! Jamie, he naughty. I want my mummy now!"

"Don't worry sweetheart," soothed Caroline, picking up Thomas and cradling him in her arms.

"Me likkle baby now," observed Thomas.

"Yes, I rather think you are," agreed Sarah with a smile "You're a wonderful, gorgeous little baby and you're mine."

She drew Thomas closer to her and he gazed at her with clear bright eyes.

"You are a real treasure, Thomas," Sarah whispered.

"Now, shall we go and do some cooking? What have I got left to do? What's left on my list? More to the point, where is my list? I'm sure I had one. Now, let's think, I know there are a few things left to do. Oh, I know. The trifle! I must whip the cream."

Just then the doorbell rang so Sarah carried Thomas straight down to the hall. James was there before her, laughing with glee.

"It's Lucy!" he cried excitedly, peering through the letter box. "It's Lucy. Lucy!"

Thomas clapped his fat hands together and joined in his brother's shrieks as Sarah opened the door.

Lucy was very flattered by the children's enthusiastic welcome and extremely amazed by the state of the hall. There were toys everywhere and she had to tread quite carefully in her high heels to avoid tripping over anything.

"Oh, you'll have to excuse the state of the place," laughed Sarah. "We've got used to it you see and once you have children there's no point in clearing up before there're in bed!"

Lucy smiled politely, but without comprehension. What did Sarah do all day, she wondered. It wasn't as if she had to go out to work. She handed Sarah a bunch of red carnations.

"I can carry, I can carry," said Thomas with great importance. Sarah let him carry the flowers in their bright yellow paper through to the kitchen.

"Careful now Thomas, there's a clever boy," she encouraged.

"I wanted to carry them," said James crossly.

"But you can hold my hand," smiled Lucy. "And what about showing me your toys?"

"Yippee!" whooped James, his jealousy forgotten in an instant. "You can play with my train set and with Hot Wheels!"

"Well, perhaps there isn't really room for the train set as well as Hot Wheels in the sitting room," said Sarah with a slightly anxious frown.

"Too late," remarked Brian cheerfully as he joined them in the hall. "James persuaded me to put both tracks out earlier this morning. Come and have a look. It's quite difficult to reach the armchairs now. Hello Lucy! I'm forgetting my manners, droning on about toy trains and cars. How are you? You're looking well! How's the teaching? Come through! How about a drink? Mind where you tread."

It was difficult to hear in the sitting room with the noise of the train set and the Hot Wheels motors but Lucy was soon settled contentedly with the children, a large glass of wine within reach.

"Are you sure I can't help?" she asked Sarah.

"Oh no! You're fine. Your job is to play with James and Thomas," laughed Sarah as she bounded back to the kitchen, hair flying.

Lucy wondered what time her sister would arrive. Caroline, Jeremy and the twins had been staying with Jeremy's brother in Putney the previous night, so it was not that far to come, but they were bound to be late, famous for it, in fact. Lucy took another sip of wine. Would she be like that, if she was married with children? Would she ever get married and have children? Would Tristan ever marry her? Would their children look like him? Would…

"Lucy, Lucy!" called James. "This is your car. See if it can go round the loop and travel under the sofa faster than mine."

Brian had set up the track for the cars and trains in a most ingenious fashion, making a feature of the lack of space in the sitting room. The cars whizzed under table legs and chairs, reappearing seconds later while the train made a steady journey around the television set, across the middle of the room, past the piano legs and then back to the television. Occasionally demented cars would fly off their tracks into the air and crash noisily.

"Mind the glasses, children," advised Brian as he popped his head round the door. "All right for wine, Lucy? Good. Won't be long now. The meal's nearly ready. Where can that sister of yours be? Not to worry. Oh, here's Sarah to chat."

Sarah flopped onto the sofa.

"I'm exhausted! I'll just sit down before making the gravy. Now, Lucy, how's it all going? How are your classes at school? Any budding musicians to encourage?"

Lucy thought grimly of some of the rougher members of Year 9. Budding musicians? Budding hooligans more likely.

"Oh, the kids are OK," Lucy said anxiously. "Some of the classes are quite easy."

"Well, don't you take any nonsense from them," advised Sarah.

"Yes," added Brian, standing in the doorway with the oven gloves still on. "Just because you're new to teaching doesn't mean you have to put up with any bad behaviour. Why, when I was at prep school, we were caned for anything, however slight."

Here we go, thought Lucy in amusement. Everyone knows about teaching because they've all been to school.

"It's probably a bit different at Springfield Comprehensive, isn't it?" said Sarah with a wink. "After all, Brian, it's over thirty years since you were at prep school!"

"Yes," murmured Brian with a faraway look in his eyes. "School days, the happiest days of your life. . . all rubbish, of course," he added cheerfully. "The happiest days of my life have been since Sarah and I got married and the kids came along."

Sarah blushed and then jumped to her feet.

"Oh, I do believe I heard a car door! Oh yes! It's them! Brian, you get the door, I'll just start the gravy and put the plates on to warm, then I'll be with you."

"Sorry to be so late, everyone," puffed Caroline as she

fought her way to the sofa, treading on bits of track and toy cars. "The traffic was terrible! And on a Sunday morning too! I don't know how you can all bear to live in London, really I don't, it's so much more civilised down in Bath where we are. Oh, a drink! Yes please Brian! Jeremy won't because he's driving. Get my bags will you Jeremy? Come on girls, in you come. Don't go all shy on me. Come on in."

Rebecca and Teresa, Lucy's nieces, edged their way into the room.

"Hello Aunty Lucy," they whispered.

"Hello you two," smiled Lucy. "Come and have a cuddle. Goodness, you've grown!"

Rebecca and Teresa were dressed in identical embroidered and sequined jeans with pink sweatshirts and very clean white trainers. Not everyone could tell them apart, but Lucy could. She pulled the twins towards her and whispered,

"We're going to have a lovely day, aren't we? Let's have lots of fun!" Turning to her sister, Caroline, she said with a smile,

"These two get more gorgeous every time I see them! And how are they getting on at school? Have they settled with their new teacher now?"

"Well," said Caroline with a frown, "their teacher, Miss Trough, says they're very lively, in fact rather wild and noisy in class. I can't quite see it myself. They're certainly not like that at home, are they Jeremy? Jeremy? Where are you?"

Jeremy appeared in the doorway, laden with bags.

"We've brought you your Christmas presents, to put away for later, just a few little things," he said to Brian. "Where do you want them?"

"Over here!" shouted James gleefully.

"Perhaps upstairs," said Brian with a grin. "And thanks very much. Come on, I'll show where we can put them and then let me pour you a drink. What was that,

Caroline? Oh, I'm sure Jeremy will be all right! It's ages until you go home and I'll make the coffee extra strong after lunch."

"Really," said Caroline with pursed lips, "Jeremy should not be drinking at all if he's driving. It's such a long journey back to Bath for us tonight and Jeremy is desperately stressed and overtired. He works so hard during the week, you know. His boss is an absolute slave driver - they all say so. And you would not believe how much paperwork Jeremy brings home every weekend. I hardly see him! It's straight up to the study, only reappearing for meals. I can hear the twins up there with him sometimes, laughing and playing, but when I go and tell them to leave their father alone he says it's all right, he can work with them in the room. I just don't understand it."

"Could you drive on the way home?" suggested Sarah. "Then Jeremy won't be so tired and he could have a drink now and relax."

"Oh no," said Caroline, looking shocked. "That wouldn't do at all! It's his job to drive us. He insists. And anyway, what about me? I always sleep on the way home, the twins too, then we put them straight to bed. Oh yes, thank you; I'd love another glass."

Lucy felt a familiar annoyance begin to sweep over her and her face turned pink as she began,

"But don't you think. . ."

"Goodness!" said Sarah, jumping up quickly, "I must finish the gravy. And come on Thomas, you need a change before lunch."

"I'll do that for you," offered Caroline. "I know where everything is. You get on with the meal. And I'll call the men down, shall I? I think they've sneaked up to the study to the computer; the twins and James must be with them."

Sarah and Caroline bustled out and Lucy was left in the chaos of the sitting room. Caroline never changes, thought Lucy angrily. She was always like that at home when we were growing up together, selfish and sanctimonious. And yet she's got everything, a beautiful home, the twins and a lovely husband. I wouldn't treat Tristan like that. He's the masterful type anyway. He wouldn't let me. He's. . . Oh, I wonder if I'll ever even see him on my own again.

Lucy busied herself tidying up cars and trains while she bit her bottom lip hard. She didn't know what was wrong these days; she was always crying and seemed so worried about everything, always thinking the worst about people and she still had to prepare next week's lessons. What a great Sunday evening that was going to be, trying to find something that could possibly hold Year 8's attention for more than five seconds. If only they'd be quiet, she knew she could teach them something. They just never let her. It was so unfair.

James put his head round the sitting room door.

"What's the matter, Lucy?" he asked in his grown up, concerned voice. "Come on, we're waiting for you at the table and you're sitting next to me! Will you eat my Brussels sprouts? I hate them and I'll be sick if Mummy makes me eat them."

"Don't worry," said Lucy with a smile. "I like them and of course I'd love to sit next to you."

Lucy stood up and smoothed down her long skirt. It will work out, she thought. I know it will! Best foot forward! Now to get through the meal. I won't let Caroline irritate me; I just won't.

"Now you have to eat some of everything," boomed Caroline's voice. "Yes, you do like carrots, Teresa. Are they organic, Sarah? But I thought I told you we only eat organic now? I know they're more expensive, but can you afford not to eat them when you consider the benefits?"

"I'm just glad when James and Thomas eat any vegetables." said Sarah with a nervous laugh. She glanced at Brian who laid a reassuring hand on hers.

"Jeremy!" shouted Caroline. "You don't put a beer glass on the table!"

"We do here," interrupted Brian firmly. "Now let's start before it all gets cold."

"Yes, do start," added Sarah. "Has everyone had mint sauce? Good. Let's tuck in."

"No want mintie sauce," sobbed Thomas.

"That's all right," soothed Sarah. "It's for grownups really. Now eat up."

Thomas put a whole roast potato in his mouth then spat it out and looked at it reflectively. He tried holding it with his fingers and biting little chunks off after that, which he found much more satisfying and delicious.

"Don't forget the meat," said Sarah to Thomas.

"Ham afterwards," he replied.

"Lamb, not ham, darling," said Brian.

"Ham," replied Thomas. "Ham, ham, ham, ham…"

"Ham, ham, ham…" shouted James with a wide grin.

"Ham, ham…" whispered Rebecca and Teresa, but they were instantly silenced by a withering glance from Caroline.

"It's a madhouse," remarked Brian cheerfully. "How's the choir going, Lucy?"

"Oh, it's great," said Lucy breathlessly and Sarah gave a quick frown, remembering that she had resolved to have a chat with Caroline about Tristan.

"I'm really glad you've joined," said Caroline to Lucy. "You need something to take your mind off the teaching, especially when you're just starting. I remember feeling quite desperate in my first teaching job - my first and last - and wondering if I would actually find the courage to turn up the next day."

"I can't imagine that," said Lucy in amazement. "You always seem to cope with everything."

"You'd be surprised what your sister was like then," smiled Sarah. "She found teaching quite a challenge, didn't you Caroline?"

Caroline nodded.

"Of course, I always said your head of department didn't give you enough support," continued Sarah. "Anyway, Lucy, Caroline was really anxious that I should get in contact with you when she knew you were moving to Springfield for your first teaching job. She was concerned that you should make a good start here and have a social life as well as work especially after her experience."

"Why, thank you, Caroline," said Lucy humbly. "And thank you Sarah too, of course, you've been great."

"I made a real pig's breakfast of my teaching," continued Caroline ruefully. "If I hadn't met Jeremy and fallen in love, I think I would have got the sack! He helped me to cope and then of course I gave up when the twins appeared, had to really, it was all too much for me."

Jeremy gave his wife a quick smile. "Double trouble, that's what twins are," he remarked cheerfully.

"Well, you should know, you're a twin too, why the stories your mother has told me about you and your brother, I could go on for hours…" began Caroline.

"That's enough of that folks!" laughed Brian. "Anyone for more wine? Good, pass your glass, Caroline. Oh, well done Thomas! You're eating your broccoli."

Thomas was holding a stalk of broccoli in his left hand and then very delicately removing the florets with the other hand and popping them into his mouth.

"Yummy!" he remarked.

"Come on girls," urged Caroline to her daughters. "You've hardly eaten anything yet! Oh please eat up!"

Just then Thomas noticed a tiny speck of broccoli on his wrist.

"Flannel!" he roared. "Flannel!"

"May I have a flannel please Mummy," corrected Sarah, as she reached over to Thomas and gently wiped his wrist with his favourite Teletubbies flannel.

"Tank you," smiled Thomas. "Tank you Mummy for

flannel. My flannel. Flannel. Flannel."

"Can I play?" shouted James. "Can I get down? Can I play? I've finished!"

"Just wait for Rebecca and Teresa," said Brian, "then you can all have a play until we call you for pudding."

"Ice cream, ice cream," yelled James. "I hope it's ice cream. Come on you girls. I want to play."

The twins dutifully bolted down the required amount of food and then melted away from the table to follow James, with little Thomas puffing along behind them, his bib still on, with bits of broccoli and lamb flying off in a shower as he ran.

"He didn't eat as much as I thought," said Sarah. "It was all in his lap!"

"Tell me more about your teaching, Caroline," said Lucy, leaning forwards, cradling her glass of wine. "You never said at home that things were difficult."

"I didn't want to say," replied Caroline. "You were still so young and of course Mum was going through such a terrible time, we all were, with Dad having died so unexpectedly only the year before, so why should I make everything worse for the family by moaning on about my own problems? Also, to be honest, I was embarrassed that I couldn't cope, so I just kept quiet. If I had asked for help sooner, I wouldn't have made such a hash of things. As it was, I only just scraped through my probationary year."

"Well, I see you in a new light now," smiled Lucy.

"I hope so!" replied Caroline. "It's tough being the big sister, you know! I was always the one who did everything first and I was supposed to set an example. Anyway, tell me more about your choir."

The two sisters chatted amicably, getting on better than they had for years, following Caroline's revelation that she had actually found something difficult. Lucy felt an unfamiliar warmth towards her sister. Should she tell her about the terrible behaviour of her Year 9 class last week, she wondered? No, better not spoil the afternoon.

Anyway, things would go better next week; they were bound to.

"And what's the chorus master like?" asked Caroline. "When Sarah first joined all those years ago, there was a rather dashing character called Tristan; everyone was madly in love with him, then he married an alto but it didn't work out. I remember you saying how good looking he was, Sarah. Why, I even think you had a crush on him!"

"Sarah!" cried Lucy in amazement.

"Oh, no," giggled Sarah, "it was just that everyone thought he was gorgeous, you know how it is. But of course he was much younger then."

Brian stood up. "I think we'll leave you three ladies to gossip about gorgeous young men while we go and clear up a bit. We could do with a bit of a break before we tackle the pudding. That lamb was delicious and I've eaten far too much! Is that OK Jeremy?"

"Of course," said Jeremy. "I'd be delighted to give you a hand."

"Well, whatever happened to Tristan?" persisted Caroline "Did he move on to better things?"

"He's still there," remarked Lucy with a blush.

"Still there," echoed Caroline disbelievingly. "Why, it must be ten years since you started in the choir, Sarah and he's still there? I thought he would have got a job with a larger choir by now, maybe one of the big London ones."

"It's twelve years since I joined the choir, actually and Tristan has been there a lot longer than that," said Sarah with a smile. "I joined as soon as I left college and then I met Brian through the choir. I think Brian had only joined to meet some girls, because he's never been that keen on singing. Anyway, once we were married and had James, Brian was happy for me to continue singing without him. Really I think he'd rather spend an evening looking after the kids than slogging through Belshazzar's Feast and sometimes I almost feel the same, but mostly I'm glad to have a bit of time to myself; it's almost the only time in the week I do, you know."

"Well, this Tristan then," continued Caroline, "how old is he then? He must be well into his forties."

"He's forty seven, actually," said Lucy. "Tristan has been conducting the choir for twenty two years now."

Caroline and Sarah looked at her in amazement.

"I worked it out from the details about him in an old concert programme," Lucy added sheepishly. "He's forty seven, that's not old, not for a man, is it?"

"It is older than twenty two," remarked Sarah gently.

Oh, so that's the way the land lies, is it, thought Caroline with interest. I'd better not say anything as I always manage to put my foot in it with Lucy. Advice from big sister is the last thing she wants, but I'll definitely have a word with Sarah later.

"Have you heard from Mum recently," asked Caroline innocently. Caroline and Lucy's mother had been widowed ten years before, when Lucy was only twelve and she had recently moved to France, a decision that had surprised the family.

"Oh yes," stammered Lucy, now brick red with embarrassment. "She's fine. She rang the other night. She seems to be having a great time in France, she's really settled there now, I suppose. Oh, excuse me a minute; I must just pop to the loo."

"Well," said Caroline excitedly when Lucy was gone. "Now tell me all!"

"It's not funny, Caroline," said Sarah. "I'm really worried about Lucy. She seems so keen on Tristan and he's such an old lecher. I mean, your sister is gorgeous, Caroline isn't she?"

"Is she?" asked Caroline. "I'd never noticed. She's not bad looking I suppose, a bit too much make up and far too thin."

"Look," said Sarah firmly, "she's a knockout and I'm worried that Tristan will take advantage of her. He's twenty five years older than she is, a very experienced man of the world and she's lonely, infatuated and struggling with her first job."

"Is she?" asked Caroline in amazement. "Oh goodness, I do begin to see what you mean. Oh Lord. Still, you can't interfere, you know; it does more harm than good. Oh goodness. Dear me. I'll have to think of something to say to her. I suppose I should really, with Mum being in France."

"Mummy! Mummy!" Piercing yells from the hall interrupted their chat. "Quick Mummy! Thomas has broken his legs!"

Sarah flew to the hall and then laughed in relief as she realised it was just another of James' little jokes.

"Got you!" shouted James, as he danced around little Thomas who was lying on the floor waving his plump legs in the air.

"Got you, got you, Mummy!" they both shouted.

"Don't tease your mother like that, boys," said Caroline sternly. "Why, if Rebecca and Teresa ever did such a thing to me. . ."

"You'd be…" began James, before Sarah silenced him with a fierce glance.

"James! Just watch it!"

"I'm going to find the twins!" James yelled, bounding up the stairs. "Twins! Here I am! Play with me! Come and see Action Man! And I've got Buzz Lightyear!"

There was some scuffling and laughter from the landing, then the sound of James' bedroom door slamming shut.

"Careful!" called out Sarah. "Mind your fingers!"

"Want to play. Want to go upstairs," said Thomas sadly.

"Come on," said Lucy, emerging from the bathroom with pink eyes. "Come on up to me and let's see if you can all play together in James' room."

Thomas puffed his way up the stairs in great excitement and tugged at Lucy's skirt.

"You are my friend," he said solemnly. "You are my best friend, Lucy."

"Pudding in five minutes," Sarah called up the stairs. "I'll put the coffee on, too."

Brian and Jeremy were staring at the computer's flickering screen in the study. They had stacked a few plates in the kitchen, then sloped off to an electronic world.

"This game really tests your skill and responses. You have to land the plane and avoid the other planes which are trying to bomb you. Here, you have a go, Jeremy."

"Thanks Brian," replied Jeremy. "I really should get this one. It's absolutely brilliant."

"Well of course, I got this for James, to develop his skills," said Brian. "Did you know that this sort of game actually develops parts of the brain that no other activity can?"

"Oh yes," said Jeremy seriously. "I'll definitely get this; the girls would love it and it would be very educational too. They spend a lot of time with me in the study, you know. They like to retreat up there when Caroline's on the warpath about something or other."

"Got a problem there?" asked Brian.

"Nothing we can't handle," said Jeremy with a grin. "Lord! This thing really goes fast. What about trying the Star Wars game next? May I have a go at that one?"

"Sure," said Brian. "Let me just find it. . ."

"There you are," wheezed Caroline as she stuck her head round the door. "We've been calling you for ages. Didn't you hear me? Boys and their toys! Hope you've enjoyed it! Come and get your pudding if you're interested. We're just about to start."

By the time the men had come downstairs, all the children were liberally smeared with ice cream and trifle.

"Yummy, yummy, yummy," said Thomas. "More please! More!"

"Just let James and Daddy have some first," said

Sarah.

Rebecca loaded her spoon with trifle and prepared to catapult it across the table at Thomas.

"Don't do that Rebecca," said James in a shocked tone of voice. "You might hit Buzz Lightyear by mistake."

Caroline turned to look at her daughter as Rebecca slid the spoon into her mouth.

"What are you doing?" she asked. "Eat up you two. Good girls."

Caroline doesn't notice anything, thought Lucy in amusement. Those two girls are going to have her running around in circles when they're older and good luck to them! Still, they're nothing like the horrors that I have to teach at Springfield High, the horrors that I've got to face first thing tomorrow morning.

Lucy pushed her plate away with the trifle unfinished. Perhaps I ought to be going home soon, she thought. Maybe if I plan each lesson in minute detail, it might just work. I could make a sort of timetable for every five minutes and then if they chat just stand there waiting until they notice. I can't bear to shout at them like some of the other teachers. It doesn't seem right. If your subject matter is interesting enough, natural discipline will follow, at least that's what they said at college. You have to trust in your own expertise and in the children's natural curiosity. Shouting and punishments are an absolute last resort. . .

"Everything all right, Lucy?" asked Jeremy who was sitting next to her. "You were miles away."

"Oh fine," said Lucy hastily. "Just doing a spot of lesson planning. I'm looking forward to another week's teaching."

"Glad it's going so well," said Jeremy. "I can't say I ever look forward to another week in the office."

"Not with your boss," said Caroline indignantly. "He takes advantage of you, Jeremy. You should stand up to him. Don't let yourself be bullied!"

"Anyone for the last spoonful of trifle?" asked Brian

with a sympathetic look at Jeremy. "No? Then what about a quick run around the garden for you kids? We've got about twenty minutes of daylight left I think. Let's make the most of it. Come on then!"

James, Thomas, Rebecca and Teresa raced to the back door with shrieks of delight.

"Me first!"

"Out of my way!"

"Last one into the garden is a banana!"

"Don't want to be a banana," wailed Thomas. "Want to be an apple."

"Boots!" shouted Sarah. "Put your boots on, children. I'm sure there are some spare ones for the girls. Just look behind the back door. . . oh, never mind. As long as they're having fun. What's a little mud, after all?"

Brian and Jeremy joined the children in the garden while Caroline and Sarah cleared the table.

"You stay there, Lucy," said Sarah firmly. "You stay and relax, unless of course you want to join the others in the garden?"

Lucy watched through the window as the children played catch with Brian and Jeremy. She didn't think her shoes could have withstood the mud outside.

"You look all in, Lucy," remarked Caroline as she bustled about with a tray. "We'll drop you at your flat on our way home. You make sure you have a nice relaxing evening before you face all those classes tomorrow. I don't envy you that at all." Then she added in a gentler voice, "Come on, love, it won't be as bad as you think."

"I'll just get my things together," said Lucy gratefully. "Sarah's been so kind having us all round, hasn't she?"

After many delays they were finally all ready to leave.

"It's been wonderful, Sarah," gushed Caroline, "and you must come down to us soon. I'll be in touch."

"Thanks for everything Sarah," smiled Lucy. "Yes, I'll see you on Wednesday at choir. Bye boys! Haven't we had fun? Yes, James, I really love Hot Wheels and Buzz

Lightyear."

As Jeremy drove through the narrow wet streets away from Sarah and Brian's house in Birdhurst Crescent, Lucy felt a surge of optimism. I know something will happen this week, she thought. I know it.

In a few minutes they were at Lucy's flat and Lucy climbed out of the car with a sigh.

"Goodbye twins," she called, making her way up the steps to the front door. "Goodbye Caroline and thank you so much for the lift, Jeremy. Have a good journey back to Bath and I hope the twins sleep all the way. Yes, see you soon! A weekend would be great, thanks."

As the car pulled away, Lucy gazed up at the dark sky and shivered.

"Oh Tristan," she whispered. "I can't wait until Wednesday when I see you at choir again. I wonder where you are now and what sort of weekend you've had."

At that very moment, Tristan was lying full length on Miss Custard Cream's sofa.

Miss Custard Cream, more properly known as Claire, had managed to persuade Tristan to allow her to cook him a vast Sunday lunch and now she was washing up while he told her all about his childhood.

"My mother was a very beautiful woman," said Tristan dreamily. "She gave me such a wonderful childhood and that's why it was such a shock when my first marriage fell apart. I did everything for my wife, everything, but in the end we had to part."

"What about marriage number two?" asked Claire a little acidly as she scrubbed at the roasting pan. "Was that someone else's fault too?"

"Oh that was such a mistake," drawled Tristan. "Such a mistake. I didn't know I could suffer that much. Now, why don't you leave those pans and come and sit down over here and stroke my forehead. I love it when you do that. Oh, your hands are a bit rough, aren't they? All that washing up, I suppose."

As Claire ran her fingers through Tristan's thinning locks, she wondered why she felt so fed up. She had been trying to get Tristan round to her flat for weeks, had worked very hard at it, in fact. Lunch had been rather disappointing as most of Tristan's conversation had been about himself or sly digs at the lack of talent shown by other musicians, particularly Miss Greymitt, the choir pianist. The attractive soprano who had sung with them at their summer concert had come in for a great deal of bitchy comments from Tristan.

"Nothing but resonance between her ears," Tristan had remarked scornfully.

Claire had tried in vain to interest Tristan in her life and concerns but he had shown no inclination to discuss her job as a legal secretary or her ambition to become an aromatherapist, beyond making one or two crude jokes about towels slipping and asking her if she would give him a full body massage after lunch.

Claire sighed and continued running her fingers through Tristan's hair. She noticed with annoyance that one of her red talons had been chipped during the washing up session. Really, roast dinners were such a pain to clear up after, it was hardly worth the effort.

"Oh Lucy," moaned Tristan. "Carry on stroking my hair; that's wonderful!"

"My name's Claire, not Lucy," shrieked Miss Custard Cream. "You know my name's Claire!"

She heard a key turning in the door as she spoke and realised with relief that her flatmate was returning.

"Now I'll have to throw you out, Tristan. It's gone five thirty and I need to get ready for the week."

"Must I go so soon?" asked Tristan regretfully. He tried to give Claire a kiss but she pushed him away as her flatmate came into the room.

"Hello! Not interrupting I hope? I'll make myself scarce."

"Don't worry," said Claire. "Tristan was just leaving."

"See you on Wednesday at choir," said Tristan with what he thought was a seductive look.

"Possibly," said Claire. "I'll see if I can manage the time."

"Never mind," said Tristan to himself with a chuckle as he climbed into his red Porsche parked outside Claire's flat. "I think this is the week that I pursue the divine Lucy in earnest. Roll on Wednesday!"

He started the engine with a roar and shot down the dark streets, passing Lucy's road on the way.

"Roll on Wednesday!" said Lucy to the night sky as she looked out of her bedroom window. "Roll on Wednesday!"

Chapter Three:
The idols and the devils

Voices grew harsher as the smoke swirled away from the smokers' corner driven by a breeze from the open window towards the non smokers.

"But surely we're here for the kid's benefit, aren't we? I mean what's the point if the kids aren't gonna learn anything? They've gotta feel we're on their side. . ."

An animated conversation was in progress in the staff room and as usual, no one was quite sure what the issues being discussed were, but opinions and beliefs were being fervently expressed.

Lucy hugged her cup of instant coffee and gazed about the room. Julia, her flatmate, flopped down beside her.

"Hi Lucy! You would not believe what sort of a morning I've had!" said Julia. "Why did Year 8 take so long to understand the past tense? I must have given them literally hundreds of examples before the penny dropped! This coffee's very welcome, I must say. Are you OK Lucy? Sorry I was in so late last night. Hope I didn't wake you. Had a nice time at Sarah's?"

"Oh yes," replied Lucy. "Great. I enjoyed seeing my sister Caroline too, which isn't always the case, as you know."

"Families!" said Julia scornfully. "Who'd choose them? Best thing is to keep right away from them if you ask me."

"Oh, families aren't bad," smiled Lucy. "Anyway, don't you want your own family one day, after you find Mr Right, that is?"

"Not interested," said Julia bluntly. "I don't know what all the fuss is about, really I don't. Why settle for one man for the rest of your life?"

"But if you fall in love..." persisted Lucy.

"You've been reading too many women's magazines," laughed Julia. "Anyway I want to get on in my career.

Don't you? I don't want to be tied down now. There's plenty of time for marriage and babies later and meanwhile I'll enjoy myself."

"Is that what you were doing yesterday evening?" teased Lucy.

"Well no, actually," said Julia. "I went to see a film then out for a pizza with Dave, you know that guy I met last week at a party, but it wasn't the most thrilling evening I've ever had. I'm not sure I'll bother seeing him again."

"Poor old Dave," laughed Lucy.

"Well, you have to meet a lot of frogs before you find your prince," remarked Julia. "And what about your love life, anyway? It's been very quiet since you moved into my flat! Time you went out with someone."

"Oh, we'll see," said Lucy secretively. "Who knows what will happen?"

"Oh look," said Julia. "There's your head of department just come in. Now have you had a word with her about your classes yet? You know how worried you were last week."

"All under control," said Lucy, but a familiar wave of nausea was sweeping over her. She hadn't said anything to her head of department, just pretended everything was fine.

Mrs Mary Goodshoe, the Head of Music, seemed to be looking for someone. With a sudden cry of delight, she spotted Lucy and made a beeline for her.

"Lucy, could I have a word?" Mary sat down heavily on the vacant armchair on Lucy's left, putting it under severe strain. "I've had a few complaints about the noise from your Year 7s this morning."

"Well, you said to do some practical music," began Lucy defensively. "There's bound to be some noise."

"Quite, quite," said Mary Goodshoe, "but nevertheless I think I might pop into some of your classes this afternoon, just to get an idea of what's going on. You never know, it might even help!" she added with a bark of laughter.

Lucy gazed at her with fascinated horror. Mary was wearing an ill fitting leaf green crimplene two piece suit and had large pieces of chocolate biscuit stuck between her top teeth. Mary laughed again, this time showering Julia and Lucy with a fine spray of biscuit.

"Yes, yes," said Lucy, edging back in her seat. "You come in at any time; I've nothing to hide!"

"Good, I'll see you later," chortled Mary, backing away from them. "Oops! Silly me! Did I tread on your toes?" she apologised to a startled maths teacher standing nearby. "I'm so clumsy, always have been," she remarked to no one in particular as she waddled off to make herself a cup of tea.

Julia and Lucy were convulsed with giggles.

"Have a biscuit Luce," offered Julia. "No? Can't think what's put you off!"

Lucy swatted Julia on the shoulder with a handy exercise book and they both started laughing again.

"Actually," said Julia, "we shouldn't be so horrible. The kids all adore Mary. She puts on a brilliant musical every summer term and for some reason manages to persuade the most unlikely characters to take part. You could do worse than ask for her help, Lucy, honestly you could. She's a born teacher, you know. Totally dedicated."

Lucy looked down at her hands and shivered. Only five more minutes until the bell.

Outside the children were enjoying their mid morning break, huddled against the side of the building to shelter from the biting wind while dipping into bags of crisps. Darren Jenkins from Year 9 was bullying a small Year 7 girl.

"Give me yer crisps," he whined. "Go on, give 'em to me!"

"Darren! Darren Jenkins! Leave her alone! Go and pick on someone your own size," shouted Mrs Goodshoe. She was standing on tiptoe, leaning out of an open window by the staff room kettle. "I've seen you! Now get yourself ready for your lessons, the bell's going soon."

Mary puffed slightly as she closed the window. She liked to keep an eye on what was happening in the playground and didn't think much of the supervision that supposedly went on. Why, these young teachers on playground duty just stood outside with their coffee and chatted. They didn't notice what was going on under their noses! She resolved to bring the matter up at the next Heads of Department meeting as a matter of urgency. You couldn't have the likes of Darren Jenkins just doing what they wanted; it wasn't right. Oh dear, thought Mary. No time for my cuppa again, still, I could just take another biscuit on the way out.

Mrs Goodshoe disappeared down the corridor with her heavy, ponderous tread. Must get the xylophones ready for my class, she thought. Or shall we sing some songs from the shows? That's it! We'll have a really good singsong, that'll cheer the kids up. It's only a single lesson, then I've got a free lesson before lunch. Let's see, I must phone the new guitar teacher and ask about exam entries for next term, then I'd better sort out my reports. . . but of course I must also remember to look in on Lucy. She'll still be teaching Year 9 as they've got double music now. She was planning to do some composing with them but I don't want to disturb her lesson if it's going well. Oh, poor Lucy. She looks thinner than ever, poor child. And she thinks I don't know what's going on! I'm just not sure of the best way to help her, don't want to just march in and take over her lessons, but really, I can't let her flounder about any longer. She's going to turn the children against music and we can't have that. With a heavy sigh, Mary unlocked her classroom door and began preparing for her lesson.

The children outside in the playground began to shuffle towards the classrooms as the bell rang, grateful that they would at least be warm for the next hour and a half. Bored, perhaps, but still warm.

As Lucy made her way back to her classroom, a feeling of desolation swept over her. How am I going to get through this term, she wondered. How am I even going to get through the morning?

Most of the class were waiting for Lucy by the time she reached the Music Department. She let them into the classroom and stood behind the teacher's desk, waiting for some sort of order to emerge.

"Good morning Year 9," she said, but they couldn't hear her over the noise. "Good morning Year 9," she yelled. "That's better, now, sit down, in silence. No, stand up, I said in silence. Yes, all of you stand up. Yes, now, oh please will you stand up? Good, now then sit down in silence, good, please keep quiet, please Year 9."

Suddenly the classroom door flew open and Darren Jenkins sauntered into the classroom. His forbidden trainers squeaked on the hard floor as he leapt over a chair and landed heavily by his desk. Lucy advanced towards him, her voice acting out the anger (or was it real anger this time?).

"Right now, just sit down now, please. We haven't got all day to wait while you stop this silly, immature way of behaving."

Darren whispered to the boy next to him who gave a coarse laugh.

"What did you say?" shouted Lucy. "If you really said what I think you said, I'll have to seriously consider sending you to the deputy head."

Darren grinned at Lucy.

"Or even to the Design and Technology Department," she ventured, knowing that among the staff of this department were some burly thickset men, the woodwork teachers, who were only too happy to "talk" to boys who had stepped out of line in her lessons.

Darren grew pale and the smirk left his face. Sensing triumph, Lucy turned to the rest of the class and told them to get their books out, as Darren had now finished wasting their time.

"Haven't got me book," piped up half a dozen voices.

"It doesn't matter, I've got some paper you can write on," said Lucy wearily. "I mean, it does matter, you should have your books, you know that, I've said that before, get yourselves organised, now come on, I'll make a list of all of you who've forgotten your books and I think your form teachers can have a look at it or am I meant to give you a detention? I can't remember, anyway, let's start, quiet please; today you're going to copy a violin and label the various parts."

"But we did that last week," remarked Darren.

"Oh, copy the 'cello then, it's on the next page in "Appreciating Music". Yes, I'm just going to give out the text books, be patient. Now, who doesn't mind sharing?"

Lucy had been going to do some composing with the class, but after complaints about the noise earlier that morning she had decided to let them do some written work for a change. It certainly made for a more peaceful lesson and she felt sure it had some educational benefit, even if it wasn't the most stimulating task the children could be asked to do.

"Now, I want you to work in complete silence and remember that I'll be taking your books in at the end of the lesson," Lucy remarked into the general hubbub of the group. As it turned out, the girls spent the lesson looking round at the boys in the class and discussing which ones they fancied and the boys spent the lesson playing computer games under their desks. Lucy was oblivious to all this, as she spent the lesson catching up with some marking that she had not found the time to do the previous evening.

None of them noticed a flash of light at the window of the classroom door towards the end of the double lesson. Mary Goodshoe was trying to find out what was going on, without undermining Lucy's authority. She was standing with her back to the classroom door, peering into the mirror of her powder compact and trying to hold it at an appropriate angle, so that the classroom would be reflected in it and she could see what was going on. Twisting the mirror this way and that in a vain attempt to get the right angle, she caught a sudden reflection of light.

"Oh bother, they're sure to have seen that," Mary gasped. Peering through the window of the door, she realised that she had not disturbed the class at all.

"Oh dear me," she whispered to herself. "Oh dear, oh dear. This won't do at all. I really will have to talk to Lucy about this. Oh dear."

Mary Goodshoe managed to catch Lucy during lunch time.

"I've cancelled choir today," she said to Lucy firmly, "so we're both free. Yes, I know it's a pity, why, I love taking choir, but needs must. We need to have a chat about your teaching."

Poor lamb, thought Mary to herself, as she led Lucy to her office. She does look tired. And I'm not going to make her feel any better by what I've got to say. Lucy's stomach gave a very loud gurgle.

"Why, haven't you eaten yet?" asked Mary in amazement. It was incomprehensible to her that anyone should skip a meal for any reason whatsoever.

"Oh, I didn't have time to make sandwiches," explained Lucy, "and I can't face the school canteen food, it's so greasy and anyway all the kids stare at me and then I can't eat."

"They're not the enemy," said Mary gently. "They're supposed to be the reason you came into teaching, something about helping them to come to a greater understanding and appreciation of music and music making as I recall from your interview. Here, you take this."

She handed Lucy a tissue and a massive wedge of her own homemade fruit cake.

"Get that cake inside you and you'll feel much better, I promise. It's because of low blood sugar levels, you know. I used to suffer from that but not now; I make sure I've got plenty of snacks to hand all the time. Perhaps I'll have a piece too; it does look so delicious, doesn't it?"

Mary spent the next half hour going over various techniques and ideas that she thought might help Lucy, patiently explaining how various methods had, in her experience, either worked or been a complete disaster for her.

"Don't have any set ideas," she warned. "Just because your tutor said something should be done a certain way doesn't mean it should be done like that in your lessons. You've got to develop your own style because that's the only thing that will work for you. And anyway," she added scornfully, "when did these tutors last set foot in a classroom? And why did they give up teaching? Something to think about, that is!"

Lucy smiled. I'm getting somewhere, thought Mary excitedly. I'm really getting through to her.

"You've got so much potential, you know Lucy," she said. "We'll get you sorted out. Now, as for this afternoon, let me see your lesson plans and I'll see if I can make any suggestions."

"Lesson plans?" asked Lucy guiltily. "Well, I certainly planned this morning's lessons, but I ran out of time for this afternoon's and anyway, what's the point? I always seem to change my mind about what I'm going to do. The classes are so difficult; sometimes they just don't let me teach."

"I know it's difficult," said Mary gently, "and of course you don't want to spend all your time planning lessons, it is the teaching that's important, but you do need to build up a repertoire of ideas and activities that you know will work. Experience will help there. But tell me Lucy, I do hope you have plenty of fun things to do outside school. What do you do with your evenings, when you're not marking homework and planning those lessons, that is!"

"Well," replied Lucy, "I've joined a local choir."

"Oh excellent!" shouted Mary, clapping her hands. "Oh what fun! Is it the Springfield Choral Society? Yes? Oh, I'm so looking forward to hearing "Belshazzar's Feast" just before Christmas."

"You're coming to that?" asked Lucy in amazement.

"Oh yes," said Mary smiling. "I have a very soft spot for that choir. Did you know I used to sing with them? No? Well I did! And sometimes I used to play for rehearsals, on the odd occasions when Miss Greymitt wasn't able to be there. I was with the choir for nearly ten years, when my boys were small. I did that and the odd bit of piano teaching, then came into class teaching in my mid thirties, when the boys were that bit older, when Michael started school in fact and of course the holidays fitted in so well. . ."

Lucy's attention began to wander as Mary outlined her meteoric rise from Assistant Teacher to Head of Music and listed most of the concerts and musicals that she had been involved in over the last twenty years.

"Anyway," remarked Mary, gathering herself up, "you've got that nice young man, Tristan, conducting the choir now, haven't you? Although I expect he's not so young now. Tempus fugit and all that!" Mary gave a snort of laughter. "Of course, Sir Digby Fork was still taking the choir when I first sang with them, now there's a real gentleman if ever I knew one; why, he was so courteous and thoughtful, if I was playing for a rehearsal, he even used to turn the pages for me in the difficult bits! But anyway, the old must give way to the new and in due course Tristan took over, shortly before I left, in fact. He was only in his mid twenties then and now here he still is, but I don't think the choir is what it was; maybe it's not his fault exactly, but things just don't seem so professional any more."

"But it is an amateur choir," said Lucy with a smile.

"You know what I mean," said Mary with another great snort of laughter. "Oh heavens, is that the time? Come on then, you run along and get yourself a coffee before your afternoon lessons. I do hope it's been helpful? Good! Off you go dear."

Lucy made her escape, thankful to be spared any more reminiscences. But how amazing, she thought, that Mary should have sung in the Springfield Chorus and even played for some of the rehearsals. She could mention that to Tristan on Wednesday if she went to the pub after choir, if he chose to speak to her. It would give her something to talk about, a common bond. She wondered what Tristan had thought of Mary. She was a competent pianist, but not brilliant and he was so rude about Miss Greymitt who was actually very good, just a little past her prime. Perhaps I won't mention Mary, thought Lucy. Tristan has such high standards. I wonder if I will ever be able to live up to them. I mean, would he really find me at all interesting once he gets to know me? OK, so I've got my music degree and so on, but when all's said and done, I'm only a teacher and not a very good one at that, whereas he, why, he's a genius! He must have done so well at college and then to go and study conducting abroad, well, he's completely out of my league! I don't know what I'm thinking of. I must be mad.

With these self pitying thoughts, Lucy reached the staff room and made herself a coffee.

"Hey Luce! Look at the notice board. Be with you in a minute!" shouted Julia.

Intrigued, Lucy made her way to the staff notice board. An evening's entertainment was planned, she read; an end of term party for the staff of Springfield Comprehensive. It was a joint party with another local secondary school, to be held at Grangewood Golf Club. There was to be a buffet supper and a live jazz band.

"Great news, isn't it?" asked Julia, appearing at Lucy's elbow. "Just what we all need to cheer ourselves up."

"Great," echoed Lucy. "Can you bring other people to the party?"

"Oh yes," answered Julia. "Look, it says here, friends and family welcome, but get your tickets soon, won't you? These parties are always very popular."

Lucy gave a secretive smile. She knew who she wanted to ask.

Somehow she struggled through the afternoon's teaching, though her thoughts wandered in a most alarming fashion.

What shall I wear to the party, she wondered. Would it be too cold for my sleeveless top with sequins? I could always wear a shawl over it but I might not need to because there will be a lot of people there and if we're all dancing, I'm very unlikely to get cold… I'd better go shopping at the weekend. I wonder if Julia would come with me to help me choose something but no, she'll start teasing me about Tristan again. It's no good asking Sarah, she's always busy with her kids and anyway, what would I end up with if she helped me chose, thought Lucy with a giggle. A nice button up to the neck blouse in taupe or beige, I shouldn't wonder!

"Miss!" yelled a hoarse voice. "Miss! Help me Miss! Me xylophone beater's got stuck between the bars again!"

Lucy rushed over to give assistance, coming back to earth with a jolt. Really, she would have to get a grip. Practical music with Year 8 demanded all her powers of concentration and endurance. A pair of ear plugs would have come in handy as well.

The last bell didn't come a moment too soon for her and she was off out of the school gates even before most of the children, much to the surprise of Mr Inchbold, the Headmaster. Mr Inchbold always kept an eye on the main exit of the school at the end of the day to watch out for those members of staff he called "slackers". Experienced members of staff sneaked out of the back entrance undetected when they wanted to leave early.

Lucy was unaware of this subterfuge and could not have been bothered with it anyway. She was on her way home. She was going to try on all her possible outfits for the party, she was going to have a long bath with a face pack and leave conditioner on her hair for at least thirty five minutes, she was going to give herself a manicure, she was going to get her Pilates book out to tone and firm her body. . . would she have time to go on a detox diet before she saw Tristan again, she wondered? Perhaps just twenty four hours on fruit and spring water would give her extra sparkle? Oh, but she had a pile of marking to do as well and she supposed she had to fill in her record of last week's teaching to give to Mr Inchbold, but she couldn't make it too truthful in case she got the sack. Year 8 practical lesson in shouting and stopping the kids breaking school music equipment wouldn't go down very well, Lucy thought in amusement, or how about Year 7 babysitting, or Year 9 desperately trying to get them to stay in their seats for more than five minutes?

I'm so fed up, thought Lucy. Why can't I teach the GCSE or A'level classes? I'd be much better with the more advanced stuff. I just don't buy this "You've got to learn to keep control first" lark from Mary Goodshoe. It's all right for her; the kids are frightened of her because she's so enormous. She could just squash them if they stepped out of line. Lucy started giggling. I mustn't be mean, she thought. Mary was trying to be really kind today at lunchtime.

"Hello Miss!" shouted Darren Jenkins, who was a few seats behind Lucy on the bus. "You gettin' off 'ere?"

"Yes I am. Hello Darren. Nice to see you."

"You live round 'ere Miss? You gotta boyfriend?"

"None of your business," said Lucy primly. "Now, if you'll excuse me."

Lucy made her way off the bus and down Stanhope Gardens to her flat. The street still showed echoes of its Edwardian elegance, although some of the front gardens could have done with a little attention. Developers were keen to buy into the street; they had already created cul-de-sacs of very expensive and tiny modern houses in neighbouring streets by purchasing several adjacent houses, flattening them and gaining access to the spacious gardens behind, but somehow Stanhope Gardens had managed to remain relatively intact.

Number 49, where Lucy and Julia occupied the top flat, had peeling light blue paintwork on the windows downstairs and new double glazed windows in Julia's flat upstairs. The front garden was home to two very compact car spaces, an assortment of dustbins, some old lumps of concrete and several large flourishing weeds.

As Lucy turned her key in the lock, her neighbour, Angela, popped her head out of the front door.

"See you in a minute, Lucy," called Angela in a cheery voice. "You're home nice and early. I'll put the kettle on - just come round when you're ready."

Of course, thought Lucy. It's Monday! I nearly forget! I said I'd start teaching little Amy the piano today.

Amy lived next door with her parents Jeffrey and Angela, her baby brother Claude and two rabbits. Angela had asked Lucy about piano lessons for Amy ages ago, in fact as soon as Lucy had moved in; Lucy was keen to teach Amy too and had been looking forward to her starting, but somehow an eventful day at school had pushed the lesson right out of her head. Lucy ran into her bedroom, dumped her school bag on the floor next to a pile of washing, picked up the piano book she had chosen at the weekend for Amy and rushed round to Number 47.

Angela welcomed her into her beautifully decorated hall and through to the living room. So this is what these houses can look like, thought Lucy in appreciation.

"You must have worked so hard on the house," she enthused to Angela.

"Glad you like it," said Angela with satisfaction. "It took ages to sand the floors and do all the painting and of course we had builders in to knock down the wall between the two rooms and so here we are now with a lovely big spacious living room."

Amy was peeping out from behind her mother's skirt.

"Hello Amy," smiled Lucy. "Look, here's your new piano book. Shall I put it on the music stand? It's got little creatures in it; aren't they sweet?"

Amy looked a bit scared when she looked at the pictures.

Goodness, thought Lucy, the friendly little creatures that I remember look like monsters now. Perhaps I should have chosen a different book for Amy.

"Would you like to sit down on the piano stool? No? Shall I? Yes, of course I'll play you something."

Lucy began playing a Chopin waltz and Amy crept up to the piano stool.

"I'll get some tea for you," smiled Angela. "That sounds so lovely. It's good to hear the piano being played properly."

By the time she returned, Amy was sitting on Lucy's knee and shrieking with laughter as Lucy tried to play a Scott Joplin ragtime piece.

"I just can't reach the left hand notes properly," laughed Lucy. "You're putting me off, Amy!"

Soon Amy was playing her first piece with Lucy accompanying her, all shyness forgotten.

"It's all middle C," said Lucy to Amy. "You're doing really well. I can hear those Red Indians dancing around in their moccasins!"

Angela watched her daughter's face from the side as Amy concentrated on thumping out her middle C crotchets. Amy's plump cheeks were flushed and her little pink tongue was touching her top lip. She gave a great whoop of joy as she came to the end of the piece.

"I can do it, I can do it!" she shouted. "I can play the piano now!"

"You've done so well," praised Lucy. "I don't think

I've ever had a pupil who enjoyed their first lesson quite so much!"

"You're the one that's done well," remarked Angela to Lucy. "You really love teaching, don't you?"

"Oh yes," replied Lucy, eyes shining. "Teaching is what I've always wanted to do, but I must say, it's not so easy with a big class. Teaching Amy now, this is a real pleasure. Now practise hard, won't you Amy? Yes, I'll see you next week for another lesson."

Lucy made her way back to Number 49 with a very light heart. Later, she was lying in the bath with a face pack on and her hair full of conditioner, still humming the Scott Joplin that had broken the ice with Amy, when she heard the telephone. Quick, she thought, it might be Tristan, I must get to the phone. She lunged out of the bath and grabbed a towel, not caring about the tidal wave of water that shot over the edge of the bath, then stopped suddenly, her heart fluttering. Oh, it can't be Tristan, can it? He hasn't got my phone number, she thought. But Deborah, your voice representative from the choir has got your number, a voice in her head insisted and she would give it to Tristan if he asked. But he wouldn't ask though, thought Lucy sorrowfully. Why on earth would Tristan want to ring me? I'm just another girl in the choir to him, nothing special.

Lucy realised that if she didn't get to that phone soon, she'd never know who it was, so she sprinted into the sitting room and snatched up the receiver.

"Hello, Lucy speaking."

"Hello, this is Steve, Steve from choir. Hello Lucy, how are you?"

"Fine," said Lucy. "Just fine. What do you want? I mean, how can I help you?"

Lucy was trying to talk very carefully without moving her lips and jaw too much as her face pack had hardened to a brittle shell and it was quite painful and awkward to open her mouth.

"I hope I haven't disturbed you," continued Steve. "Have I interrupted your meal? You sound, well, not like you usually do! Are you OK?"

"Fine, fine," mumbled Lucy. "Everything's fine. I was just having a bath and had to run to the phone, that's all."

"Well," said Steve, "the reason I rang was to ask if you are going to the party at Grangewood Golf Club, the one for your school and mine; have you heard about it?"

"Yes, I think I'll go," said Lucy.

"Great," enthused Steve. "Make sure you get your ticket early, won't you? Or maybe you'd like me to get you a ticket? My treat. The jazz band that's playing is really fantastic. I know one of the band members; he's an old college friend of mine. You'll really enjoy it."

"Oh, I'll get my tickets, don't you worry," said Lucy firmly.

"Tickets?" echoed Steve. "Oh, I expect you're bringing one of your friends, great idea, the more the merrier. Lucy, I hope you don't mind me ringing like this, but I just wanted to make sure you got a ticket."

"That's all right," said Lucy, rather surprised.

"See you on Wednesday at choir," said Steve. "Have a good time until then."

"Oh, I'm really looking forward to choir," cried Lucy, forgetting about her face mask and feeling a sudden stab of pain as the dry mask pulled on her face. "Goodbye Steve. Roll on Wednesday!"

"Goodbye," said Steve softly. His hands were sweating slightly as he put the phone down. He had wanted to ask Lucy to go out with him this weekend but perhaps it was a bit too soon. She had sounded slightly unfriendly on the phone at first, anyway. I expect she's tired, he thought and anyway choir is only two days away. Perhaps she'll go to the pub afterwards. We'll see. Roll on Wednesday indeed.

Lucy felt the hair conditioner dripping down her neck as she stood wrapped in her towel on a slightly soggy patch of carpet next to the phone. I'm surprised Steve rang, she thought, just to ask about the party. I didn't even know he had my number. He must have asked Deborah at choir for it. I wonder if he's keen on me, Lucy thought with a giggle. Oh, why couldn't Tristan have phoned? I'm going to have to pluck up the courage to ask him to the party at Grangewood Golf Club. I wonder what he'll say? Goodness, I'm ruining Julia's carpet, standing here. I'd better get back to the bathroom and finish attempting to make myself look beautiful.

When Lucy was asleep that night, Tristan came to her dreams as usual. She reached out for him, but there seemed to be something in the way.

"What is it? Where's Tristan?" Lucy wondered aloud. A vast pile of exercise books seemed to be blocking her way to Tristan, a heap of books about twenty feet high. There was something large moving under the books.

"What is it? Who is it?" she murmured. Some of the books gently floated away and Lucy could see Steve sitting at a desk and smiling at her, seeming not to mind the weight of all the paper on him. Amy drifted past with her piano book, dancing delicately to a Chopin waltz. She pirouetted on top of the books and then they all cascaded down, pushing Steve away out of sight and revealing Tristan behind.

"Tristan, oh Tristan!" called Lucy. But this was not the Tristan she knew. This one was snarling at her, enraged and bellowing like an ancient bull fighting his last fight. His face came nearer and Lucy backed away in terror. The exercise books reappeared. They began falling from the sky like rain, falling, falling and covering Tristan little by little until he was completely obscured, the final book landing with a satisfying thwack. Lucy looked at the cover of the book and read,

"Your presence is requested at the marriage of Miss Lucy Lavender and Mr Scott Joplin. The wedding breakfast will be served at Grangewood Golf Club with the Blue Sunset Band providing the music. Carriages at dawn."

Curiouser and curiouser thought Lucy as she turned over. Curiouser and curiouser.

Chapter Four: Sing Joyfully

Steve and Lucy both arrived at choir early on Wednesday, Steve so that he could sit in the front row of the basses and gaze at Lucy and Lucy so that she could sit in the front row of the sopranos and gaze at Tristan. The two of them collided on the steps leading up to the rehearsal hall and looked at each other in surprise.

"He, Hello," stammered Steve. "How are you, Lucy? You look wonderful, I mean you look well."

"I'm fine," said Lucy with a frown. "Now, I must get in and save my place, so if you'll excuse me."

Lucy was off before Steve could say anything else. He followed her into the hall and watched as she plonked her coat on two chairs in the front row and rushed off to the ladies. The hall was virtually empty, cold and unwelcoming. Not all the lights had been switched on yet and Miss Greymitt was sitting at the piano softly practising the accompaniment in her fingerless mittens, peering intently at the music.

"Oh bother!" she exclaimed. "My eyesight just isn't what it used to be!"

"Would you like me to switch more lights on?" asked Steve.

"Thank you young man. Stephen, isn't it? Yes? I seem to remember you from your audition."

"Yes," said Steve, looking embarrassed. "I wasn't quite at my best that day. Frog in the throat, you know. Probably nerves."

"I thought you sang beautifully," said Miss Greymitt firmly. "I don't suppose you'd mind turning the pages for me, would you, while I practise this difficult bit? You really need three hands for this!"

"Not at all," replied Steve and he followed the music as Miss Greymitt played, turning one bar before the end of the page, when she gave him a vigorous nod.

"And the next turn too, if you wouldn't mind?" she

asked breathlessly as her hands scampered up and down the keyboard.

"This really is a fiendish section of Belshazzar, but such wonderful music! Of course, I met the composer, Sir William Walton, once. Such a distinguished looking man with such a beautiful wife."

Steve's attention was drawn away from Miss Greymitt at that point, as Lucy returned from the ladies.

Wow, thought Steve as he gazed at her. She is beautiful.

At that moment, Sarah rushed through the door wearing her beige anorak, her umbrella turned inside out and her hair windswept and dripping with water. Why is Lucy wearing that glittery stuff on her eyelids, Sarah wondered. And why is she wearing so much pink lipstick? It makes her mouth look so big. Sarah shook her head in disbelief, scattering water on the wooden floor.

"Turn, turn," said Miss Greymitt frantically as Steve gazed at Lucy. "Stephen! Where are you? Turn the page!"

"Oh sorry," replied Steve. "Got to go now."

Steve rushed over to Lucy and began chatting animatedly to her about his classes that afternoon and about how much marking he had. What am I saying, he thought with a groan. Why can't I just act normally?

"What's that bleeping sound?" asked Lucy in alarm. "Is it a phone? It doesn't sound like a phone."

"That's my electronic organiser," said Steve proudly. "Look, do you want to see what it says? It's reminding me to mark Year 10's books by tomorrow. They had to find out about Oliver Cromwell, you know."

"Great," said Lucy vaguely. "Make sure you switch the alarm off for the rehearsal, won't you? Tristan will go mad if you disturb him when he's working. He was furious last week with that tenor who left his mobile phone on in and quite justifiably so in my opinion."

"Tristan was outrageously rude, you mean," laughed Steve. "He couldn't have been more sarcastic if he'd tried.

It was a simple mistake, to leave your phone on and if he'd been in a better mood, Tristan would have seen the funny side of it. These temperamental musicians!"

Lucy did not respond to Steve as she was gazing with rapt attention over his shoulder. Tristan had just arrived, his long raincoat hanging carelessly over his shoulder and his dark curls glistening from the rain. Miss Custard Cream came in behind him.

"Claire," Tristan drawled. "Thought you weren't coming this week?"

"Oh, nothing better to do, you know how it is," she replied with a smile. "See you later in the pub."

Claire had decided to give Tristan another chance. Perhaps she had just been having an off day last Sunday and he really was so good looking. Claire quickly grabbed the last place in the front row, moving Lucy's coat and sitting down next to her.

"You can't sit there," snapped Lucy. "I mean, should you sit there? I'm a first soprano and you're only a second, aren't you? I might put you off. And besides, I've saved that seat for my friend Sarah."

"I don't suppose I will hear you at all," retorted Claire. "My own voice is very full and powerful, you know. Anyway, the choir doesn't divide that much in this piece."

"Yes it does," answered Lucy angrily. "If you sit here, the whole balance will be wrong. Besides, I'm in the semi chorus as well."

"So am I," said Miss Custard Cream smugly. "And I need to sit near the front to see properly and I can't bear all the talking that goes on in the back row. I'm here to sing."

I doubt that very much, thought Lucy, really annoyed. She had hoped to save a seat for Sarah but it was too late now.

Lucy smiled apologetically when she saw Sarah making her way over to the soprano section, looking nervously for a seat. I must remember to thank her for last

Sunday, thought Lucy. It was so kind of her to have us all round.

"Can we begin, ladies and gentlemen?" asked Tristan. Let's stand and do some exercises. Blow the cobwebs away! When you're ready, Miss Greymitt."

As the choir ran through their warm up exercises, Lucy felt herself getting extremely hot. She was sandwiched between Claire and Deborah, her voice rep, both of them singing with great gusto, if not great accuracy. Deborah was moving to her left a little each time she took a breath and poor Lucy was beginning to feel rather squashed. The situation was not eased that much when they sat down, as Deborah needed a slightly larger chair to accommodate her ample hips.

"Could you move your chair over a bit please Deborah?" asked a soprano in the row behind. "It's just that I can't quite see Tristan. You're blocking my view."

"Sure," answered Deborah. "Is that better?"

She eased her chair to the right and Lucy turned round and gave a grateful smile to the soprano in the row behind them. To her amazement, she saw that it was Angela, her next door neighbour, her pupil Amy's mother.

"Hello!" Lucy whispered. "Hello Angela! I didn't know you were joining the choir."

"Well, I thought I'd give it a go," whispered Angela. "I know you must be surprised!"

"Ladies! Will you stop talking?" boomed Tristan.

"See you in the break," mouthed Angela as Lucy turned back.

During the coffee break, Lucy chatted to Angela and Sarah, introducing them to each other.

"This girl's a wonderful teacher, you know," said Angela to Sarah. "She's just started teaching my daughter Amy the piano and Amy can't wait for her next lesson."

"Well I hope I don't put her off in the second lesson," smiled Lucy.

"So what made you join the choir?" Sarah asked

Angela.

"I'd been thinking about getting out and doing something for ages, but you know how it is when you're busy with a family, anyway, I applied for an audition with the Springfield Choral Society shortly after Lucy moved in because she told me what fun it was! I thought it would take ages for my application to be processed, which is why I didn't say anything to you, Lucy and I never actually thought they'd want me, but apparently you need more sopranos for Belshazzar, so I was asked to audition at very short notice yesterday and here I am! I can hardly believe it! I'll have to do some note bashing at home, though, to catch up with the rest of you. I'm relying on you to help me, Lucy! I don't even know where the first note is on the piano!"

Angela gave a shriek of laughter and Sarah joined in, braying and nodding in agreement.

"Lucy!" came an urgent voice behind her. "Lucy!"

Lucy turned round to see Steve behind her.

"Fancy going to the pub afterwards?" he asked. "A group of us are going; it should be fun."

"Oh yes," said Lucy gratefully. She wanted to go to the pub to have a chance to talk to Tristan, but she wasn't sure she wanted to go with Sarah again this week. If she went along with a whole group of people it would be easy to slip away to chat to Tristan and if he was busy she could always just rejoin the group.

"Yes please," repeated Lucy. "That would be great. See you afterwards."

Steve made his way back to his seat with a light heart. He was really getting somewhere with Lucy, he knew it! He checked his electronic organiser quickly when he sat down; it was reminding him to ask Lucy out, possibly for Saturday if she could make it. He might suggest they went out to see a film, or perhaps out for a meal, or even both. He looked across at Lucy. She was looking gorgeous, with her long hair falling across one shoulder in a golden red sheet as she leant forward to pick up her music. She's the girl for me, he thought. I just adore her.

After the rehearsal was over, he waited by the door for her.

"Where are the others?" she asked with a frown.

"Others?" echoed Steve. "Oh, no one else wanted to go for a drink tonight, I suppose because it's midweek and the weather's pretty foul."

"Perhaps I should go home," said Lucy sadly. "It's not really sensible to go out in the middle of the week."

"Nonsense," said Steve, taking her firmly by the elbow. "Let's go for a drink. Would you still like to? Good. Come on then. And you can tell me all about your classes."

Why would anyone want to know about my classes wondered Lucy. When I'm not at school I try to forget about them. They make me feel so depressed. I'd really like to teach some of those kids, but it's as if there's a brick wall stopping me getting through to them.

"What are you thinking, Lucy?" asked Steve, as they made their way along the street, shivering in the cold wind. Car headlights were reflected in the shiny windows and glass doors of the office blocks as they hurried past.

"Oh, I was trying not to think about school, you know," laughed Lucy. "I think about work when I'm there and try to forget it and have a good time when I'm away from it. It's my way of surviving the term."

"Surviving?" asked Steve with a frown. "Surviving? Is it that bad?"

"Yes," said Lucy abruptly, "so let's change the subject. Here we are at the pub."

They turned down a narrow side street and could hear the clink of glasses and the sound of raucous voices as they approached. Despite the weather, several of the basses were standing outside the pub with their beer, laughing and joking.

"Here's Steve," they shouted. "Steve! Come and join us! Or are you busy?"

"Another time," smiled Steve as he pushed the pub door open to let Lucy go in first. One of the basses winked at Steve as he went in.

"Lucky old Steve," the bass commented. "And we all thought Tristan was after that one."

The pub was warm and muggy, with the smell of beer overlaid with crisps. Lucy wrinkled her nose in distaste.

"How about me taking you to a nice country pub sometime?" asked Steve. "It might be a bit more pleasant than this one."

"Oh great," said Lucy dreamily, looking round to see if she could see Tristan. "Is Tristan here yet? Can you see him?"

Was that a yes or a no, wondered Steve. I can't tell what she's thinking. Sometimes I wish I knew more girls, then I might know what's going on in their heads.

"Look, I can see Tristan," said Lucy excitedly. "He's just come in with a group of people."

"Yes, there he is," said Steve. "And I see that Claire's still trailing after him."

"Are they, you know, well, are they going out together?" asked Lucy.

"I don't think "going out" is quite the right phrase," said Steve with a laugh."Tristan was definitely interested in her last summer, made quite a play for her before the concert in fact, but then I think he got rather distracted by the visiting soprano soloist who sang with us that evening. Then again, you never can tell with Tristan. He'd go after anything in a skirt, that's what the other chaps in the basses say!"

Steve doesn't know Tristan very well, thought Lucy. Just because a man's good looking doesn't mean he's a womaniser. I expect there are always silly rumours flying around about conductors and I'm sure Tristan's not interested in Miss Custard Cream. The very idea! She's making a fool of herself running after him. She has no idea how ridiculous she's being and anyway that top she's wearing doesn't suit her at all. It's far too tight and the wrong colour for her entirely. You have to be very careful with fuchsia pink.

Lucy doesn't know Tristan very well, thought Steve. What a very sentimental idea she has of the man. I suppose, being a musician herself, she admires his musical talent. Perhaps she'd like to conduct a big choir one day. That would explain her interest in him.

"Shall we go and join the others at the bar?" asked Lucy brightly, looking at Tristan and his entourage.

"I expect you'd like to discuss different styles of conducting or choice of music, wouldn't you?" asked Steve in a kindly voice. "You see, I've guessed your secret!"

"Have you?" asked a bewildered and red faced Lucy.

"You're after his job, aren't you?" said Steve. "Oh, not now, but a few years down the line. Don't be embarrassed; it's great to have ambitions."

"Well I'm not sure that I want to stick at classroom teaching," smiled Lucy, relieved, "not that there's anything wrong with it," she added hastily as Steve looked a bit discouraged. "It just doesn't feel like me, that's all, but I really love music."

"Oh look, you could grab that table," said Steve, deftly steering Lucy towards a cosy corner of the pub. "I'll get you a drink; won't be a tick."

Tristan noticed Lucy sitting on her own in the corner and looked her up and down. She caught his gaze and he narrowed his eyes slightly to focus better on her face. I can't quite make out her expression, thought Tristan vaguely. I suppose I should be wearing those glasses that the optician said I needed, damn fool that he is!

"We all need a little help with age, Mr Proudfoot," the optician had told Tristan. "You should wear your glasses all the time now. You don't want to strain your eyes now, do you?"

Strain my eyes? What utter rubbish. I don't need glasses, Tristan thought. They wouldn't look right on me.

The pair I tried on in the opticians made me look positively decrepit. It's just a little bit smoky in here, so I can't see properly.

Tristan squinted at Lucy again to try to see her clearly. I'll go over to her, he thought and have a little chat.

He's moving over to me, thought Lucy in a sudden panic. Tristan's going to talk to me.

"Hello Tristan," she whispered as he slid into the seat beside her.

"You're looking gorgeous tonight," Tristan murmured, gazing deep into her shiny eyes and catching a reflection of himself as she looked straight at him. "Utterly, utterly gorgeous."

"Oh, thank you, I suppose," said Lucy, utterly scarlet.

"I'll come straight to the point, sweetie," said Tristan. "Stupid to beat about the bush at my age." He gave a harsh laugh as he took a long slow drag of his cigarette.

Why do musicians smoke, thought Lucy, annoyed. Don't they know anything? He needn't think he can do that when we're married.

"Will you let me take you out to dinner soon?" Tristan whispered hoarsely. "Say Friday, the day after tomorrow?"

Lucy nodded joyfully, unable to speak.

"Quick then, give me your phone number. I'll give you a ring tomorrow and arrange things. Well, I must say, I'm looking forward to this already," leered Tristan as he staggered back to the bar where his groupies were standing. They were looking angrily at Lucy and wondering what Tristan had been saying to her.

"What's Tristan looking forward to?" asked Steve in amusement as he got back to the table with a white wine for Lucy and a beer for himself. "He's already had a bit too much alcohol in my opinion. Now Lucy, you know you said you'd like to go out for a drink with me, well, what about this Saturday or Sunday?"

"Did I? When did I? Oh, yes, I suppose I might have said something, but I'm sorry Steve, I'm going to stay with my sister Caroline this weekend. She lives down in the West Country, in Bath and I promised I'd stay this weekend. My nieces are dancing in their end of term show and I couldn't miss that."

"Not to worry," said Steve, disappointed that he wouldn't see Lucy at the weekend. "Actually, I should go and stay with my parents this weekend; it's my Mum, she's not at all well, in fact she's been ill for ages." Steve's voice faltered away.

"What's wrong?" asked Lucy in sudden concern.

"Well, she's had cancer, she's terribly brave you know and we're all optimistic; I'm sure she'll be all right, the doctors are wonderful and they caught the cancer very early on, but the treatment has made her feel so wretched you see, so tired, so I really try to help out. It's my dad too, of course, he needs all the support he can get."

"And where is home," asked Lucy gently.

"Not far, only about ten miles away, Bakesville. Do you know it? A little village."

Lucy nodded.

"I try to get home once or twice during the week and have a longer visit at the weekend. And what about you, Lucy? Do you see your parents a lot?"

"No," said Lucy. "Dad died ten years ago."

Steve nodded sympathetically.

"Mum misses him like mad, well, we all do, although sometimes I think I can hardly remember him, it seems so long ago. Anyway, Mum has let the house in Bath where Caroline and I grew up and she's moved to the south of France. She says it's a permanent move, but I'm not so sure. She hasn't sold the house in Bath, so she could easily move back."

"Poor you," said Steve. "You must miss your dad. Will you go out to France for Christmas?"

"Maybe, but I might go and stay with my sister, Caroline. Have you got brothers and sisters, Steve?"

"Yes. Twin sisters."

"Twins! Oh how wonderful!"

"Not always," said Steve with a laugh. "You should try growing up with twin sisters bossing you about!"

"My sister Caroline's got twins, my two little nieces," said Lucy. "I've always thought that I'd like to have twins, that is, when I, if I ever get married," Lucy added with a blush.

She's perfect, thought Steve, so sweet and lovely.

"Well, what about going out on Friday," asked Steve. "I usually do some marking then but I could fit it in some other time."

"Oh no," said Lucy in confusion. "I mean, I didn't say, well, you see I'm already going out them, it's only just arranged you see, oh dear, I didn't mean to mislead you; I'm already going out on Friday, to dinner with Tristan."

"Tristan," echoed Steve in disbelief. "Tristan," he said a little louder.

Tristan turned round when he heard his name and looked blankly in their direction but, unable to place the sound, he soon turned back to Claire.

"I really enjoyed the meal you cooked on Sunday," Tristan whispered to Claire. "How about getting together again this weekend?"

On the other side of the pub, Steve was covered in confusion.

"Oh," he said to Lucy. "I've been very foolish, I'm sorry Lucy, I thought. . . oh, never mind."

Too late, thought Steve bitterly. Too late, that bastard Tristan's after her. How can she be taken in by that creep?

Steve turned round to look at his rival and saw Tristan leering at Claire over yet another large whisky. No, thought Steve, it won't do. It won't do at all. Lucy's worth more than this. Tristan will never be serious about anyone; he's just after another notch on his bedpost.

"Are you sure you know what you're doing?" Steve asked Lucy sharply. "Tristan's got quite a reputation you know and look how he's behaving with Claire! Just think about it Lucy; don't be an idiot!"

"I know what I'm doing," said Lucy indignantly. "I'm not a child. It's only dinner. He's just asked me out to dinner. And I've been hoping he would for so long."

"OK, OK," hissed Steve grimly. "Lecture over. It's your life. You do what you want."

Inside, Steve was shaking and furious. That complete, complete bastard, he thought. Lucy's my girl, or so I thought. Tristan doesn't really want her, whereas I, I, why, I think I'm in love with her! Well I'm not giving up, not at all. If Tristan wants a fight he can have one!

Steve looked at Lucy and tried to smile.

"Have I told you about the project I'm doing with Year 7? It's all to do with the Middle Ages and we're having a great time doing the research for it."

Lucy glanced at her watch, having heard all she wanted to about Year 7's project.

"I should be going," she said. "School tomorrow!"

"I'll give you a lift," said Steve, "that is, if you'd like me to. Would you like a lift?"

"I'm all right on the bus," said Lucy politely. Really, she thought, I don't want to encourage him any more. It isn't fair.

"Oh, I insist," said Steve. "It's freezing out there and probably raining by now. It's just a lift! I promise I won't get the wrong idea."

"All right," said Lucy laughing. "I give in! Take me home!"

Lucy looked around for Tristan as she left, but he was still in deep conversation with Claire at the bar, telling her about his trip to Bayreuth in his early twenties.

"Marvellous, simply marvellous," drawled Tristan. "The best experience of my life, well, nearly the best, if you know what I mean!" He gave one of his harsh laughs and tossed his few remaining curls over his shoulders. Steve led Lucy back to his rather battered red Volvo that was parked in a side street near to the pub.

"This was as close as I could get to the rehearsal hall," he explained. "Honestly, parking in Springfield has become a complete nightmare with all these red routes they're putting in. Do you drive, Lucy?"

"Well, I can drive, but it's not worth me getting a car yet, after all, there's a good bus route to town from where I live and it's easy to get to school too."

"You're much safer in a car, you know, especially at night," said Steve frowning.

"Depends how you drive," laughed Lucy. "Come on, let's get in; I'm freezing!"

Steve opened the door for Lucy and she climbed in and sat down on an untidy heap of test papers.

"Oh bother," said Steve. "I suppose I ought to mark those when I get back to the flat. Just chuck them on the floor, would you Lucy?"

"Are you sure?" asked Lucy. "Look, I'm going to put them on the back seat. It's cleaner there for them. After all, your pupils have put a lot of effort into those tests, haven't they?"

Steve said nothing but merely raised his eyebrow as he pulled his seatbelt over his chest. Lucy started to giggle and soon they were both laughing helplessly. As Steve pulled away from the kerb he said,

"Actually, most of my pupils think that revising for a test is just a matter of glancing at their notes as they walk into the classroom. They haven't got a clue about hard work but that's what I'm there for I suppose," he continued cheerfully, "to show them what to do and how to do it. Now, which way should I be going at this junction?"

"I hope I'm not taking you out of your way," murmured Lucy. "It's right at the lights, then round the station and straight on. I live in Stanhope Gardens; do you know it?"

"I think so," said Steve. "I think I may have driven past once or twice and of course I don't mind going out of my way. I actually live over the other side, quite near my school, Fairfield High. It's just a little flat, but it's mine, or at least the building society's!"

And this way, thought Steve joyfully, I can find out where you live.

Steve had already decided to send Lucy flowers tomorrow. He wasn't quite sure why women liked flowers so much but his sisters had told him many years ago that flowers always made a difference and he was pleased to be able to put this knowledge to good use. This would be the real beginning of his campaign to woo Lucy; there was no way he was going to let Tristan win!

There was a light on in Lucy's flat when they drew up outside number 49.

"That's it, up there," pointed Lucy. "Julia must be home. She's a teacher at Springfield High too; French is her subject. She's been a really good friend to me and the rent is very reasonable."

"See you soon," murmured Steve softly. "Here, let me help you with the seat belt; I think it's stuck."

"No, it's fine," said Lucy cheerfully as she bounded out of the car. "See you Steve! Thanks!"

"Good evening?" asked Julia as Lucy came into the flat.

"Blissful!" said Lucy. "I'm going out to dinner on Friday with Tristan. What shall I wear?"

"Let's go and see," said Julia eagerly and the two of them rushed off to Lucy's wardrobe to have a good look.

"Are you going to wear your hair up? No? I suppose you're right, it's too formal, but at least you'd look a bit older. People might think he's your dad otherwise! Oh, sorry Luce, it's only a joke. Look, I'll go and make us a drink. All right?"

Lucy nodded feverishly, pulling at her clothes in the wardrobe. How on earth could she decide what to wear? She didn't even know which restaurant he was taking her to yet. After about ten minutes, she had found two possible outfits and hung them up in her room from the picture rail. She could try them on tomorrow and decide then, because now she really needed to have her bath and get to sleep. She had to look her best for Friday.

Julia brought her a mug of herbal tea.

"I've made camomile tea; it's supposed to be relaxing so you enjoy that in your bath and for heaven's sake, calm down Lucy! You won't get any sleep otherwise."

But Lucy did sleep well, like a baby, she thought to herself as she lay in bed in the morning, happy that this was the day that Tristan was going to phone her. Not that babies sleep particularly well, Lucy thought idly, at least Caroline always said that Rebecca and Teresa were terrible at night and didn't sleep for more than a couple of hours between feeds, but anyway my babies will probably sleep well. Lucy giggled and turned over then shot out of bed with a shriek.

"Julia! Julia! Why didn't you wake me? It's 7.30! We're going to miss the bus at this rate!"

"I was just leaving you to dream about your beloved," called back Julia. "If you hadn't got up in the next ten minutes, I would have given you a shout, honestly!"

Lucy and Julia managed to get to work on time, in fact with a few minutes to spare.

"That was cutting it a bit fine," laughed Lucy. "We were very lucky that a bus came along so quickly!"

"You've got a bounce in your step this morning, Lucy!" remarked Mary Goodshoe when she saw Lucy in the Music Department, getting ready for her classes.

I wonder what's going on, thought Mary. I do hope Lucy isn't going to be distracted from her work. Maybe she's found her feet in the classroom at last. A quick peek through Lucy's classroom window at 10 am, however, told Mary that this wasn't the case. Lucy was sitting at her desk smiling and gazing into the distance while her year 8 class were tearing pages out of their music exercise books and flicking them at each other.

Meanwhile, at Fairfield High School, Steve was ordering Lucy flowers during a free lesson.

"Something colourful, I think," Steve suggested to the florist. "I'm not sure what's in season in the winter."

"Leave it to us, sir," said the florist firmly. "I think I know what would be suitable. And the message is to read?"

"Message?" echoed Steve. "Oh, "From an Admirer", I think, yes, "From an Admirer", that's it."

One of Steve's sisters had been sent flowers "From an Admirer" once and she had seemed pleased with them. It sounded like the sort of romantic stuff that women liked and had an air of mystery to intrigue her. At least she'll know they're not from Tristan, thought Steve, because his tightfistedness is legendary. Tristan would do anything to avoid buying a round in the pub, or so Steve had heard from the other basses. Yes, thought Steve happily, Lucy is bound to guess that the flowers are from me and I'm sure she'll think better of me for it.

The bouquet of flowers arrived at 49 Stanhope Gardens at six o'clock that evening.

"Miss Lucy Lavender?" enquired the delivery girl.

"Yes, that's me," said a beaming Lucy. "Ooo! How gorgeous!"

"Someone's keen," remarked the girl. "Here's the card."

"From an Admirer," read Lucy. Well, I know who that is, she thought as she ran up the stairs two at a time with the huge fragrant bouquet quite filling her arms. She cradled the flowers almost as if they were a small child.

"Now, which vase shall I use? Where are the scissors? I think they'd look best in the sitting room, no, the bedroom, definitely the bedroom. Hmm, they smell heavenly."

As Lucy buried her face in the flowers, the telephone

rang.

"It's Tristan," drawled a familiar voice. "Tristan Proudfoot. Is that you, Lucy? You see, I promised I'd ring."

"Oh, hello," whispered Lucy. "Hello Tristan."

"Now, what about dinner," he continued. "Shall I pick you up at about 8pm?"

"As late as that? I mean, yes, of course, whatever you want," said Lucy, still amazed that she was actually talking on the phone to the man of her dreams.

"Well, seven if you prefer sweetie; that gives us more drinking time, doesn't it?"

"Thank you, thank you for the flowers," gushed Lucy.

"Oh great," said Tristan vaguely. Had he sent Lucy flowers? He didn't think so, but he had had quite a hangover all morning and anything was possible. No, he knew he hadn't sent her flowers; he would have remembered. This was ridiculous.

"There're so lovely," gushed Lucy. "I really adore flowers. It's so generous of you."

What the hell, thought Tristan.

"Glad you liked them," he said. "And see you tomorrow, looking as gorgeous as ever! Bye!"

Lucy stood looking at the phone for ages after the call, perfectly, perfectly happy. So this love, she thought. Phone calls and flowers. It's all starting for me now.

Chapter Five: Rejoice and drink

Friday passed in a blur for both Lucy and Tristan; for Lucy because she was so full of joyful anticipation of her dinner with Tristan and for Tristan because he was suffering from yet another of his hangovers.

"I drink to forget," he grumbled sorrowfully to himself. "I drink to forget the way women have treated me. If only my mother had treated me differently and as for my first wife, why that bitch. . ."

Tristan's mind went blank at this point and he couldn't really remember what his first wife had done wrong; all he could remember was a very young scared looking girl with long red hair, gazing at him with love in her eyes as she advanced down the aisle on her father's arm to join him at the altar. Oh, why didn't it work out, thought Tristan wretchedly. Why couldn't she give me more space, more freedom? She didn't understand me or any man really. Just for a moment a tiny doubt entered Tristan's mind. Could he have contributed to his marriage breaking up? But no, that was silly. He hadn't done anything wrong, well, nothing that his wife hadn't driven him to, anyway. As for his second wife, he couldn't think about that at all, no, it was far too painful. Never again, he shuddered, I will never ever marry again. Women only want to trap you and use you as a meal ticket for them and a string of brats. No thank you! He had seen his first wife once up in London, with her new husband and a little toddler, outside the Natural History Museum. They had looked very cosy, both of them obviously besotted with the child. Tristan had felt a wistful pang of something, he wasn't quite sure what. That could have been me, he had thought, staring at his ex-wife's new husband. But no, I'm a genius, a musical genius, I have my career and I'm cut out for a more bohemian lifestyle. What do I want with family life and prams and all of that stuff? Tristan had walked on quickly in case they had seen him, but couldn't resist a quick glance over his shoulder. His ex-wife had looked up at her new husband, her face shining with adoration. Why, Tristan had thought crossly, she's cut her hair short and I'm sure she's put on weight. No, wouldn't have done for me at all.

Tristan fell asleep on his sofa at this point and spent the afternoon snoring noisily amidst the wreck that was his sitting room. His grand piano was open with the lid up and piles of music were strewn everywhere, mixed with CDs, unopened bills and the odd coffee cup and ash tray. He woke up again at six o'clock.

"Another drink, I think," Tristan announced to the empty room, "before I get ready to collect the divine Lucy! And I suppose I'd better clear up some of this junk, in case I bring her back for coffee."

Tristan leered at himself in the mirror and ran his tongue over his dry lips. Actually, he thought, I'd prefer a pot of tea. I feel so thirsty, can't cope with the booze the way I used to and perhaps I need to sober up anyway. I want to make an impression on young Lucy.

Tristan shuffled into his kitchen to put the kettle on and wondered if he had time to have a shower before he went out.

Lucy went straight to her wardrobe on her return from school. She rejected the two outfits she had chosen the previous night out of hand. How could I have thought they were suitable, she wondered. No, I want to look sophisticated but naturally glamorous for Tristan. I want to look as if I've just thrown on the first thing I found in the wardrobe but look like a supermodel as well.

After soaking in a long bath and trying on lots more clothes, Lucy finally settled on a smart pair of black trousers with a fitted turquoise top and long turquoise earrings, which was one of the outfits she had originally picked out the day before. The doorbell rang as she put on the matching black jacket. Lucy stared at herself in the mirror. This is it, she said to herself. He's here.

Lucy opened the door nervously, preparing herself to see Tristan's face.

"Hello Lucy! Hope we're not disturbing you!"

It was Amy and her mother Angela from No. 47 next door.

"I wanted to ask whether you could help me with the notes of Belshazzar sometime? I don't want to bother you - oh, you're all dressed up too! Going anywhere nice? With anyone nice?"

"I'm not sure where we're going, actually," answered Lucy. "I forgot to ask. But, yes, I am going with someone nice."

"That good looking young man Steve, is it?" teased Angela. "I thought he seemed keen."

"No, it's…" began Lucy and then she broke off in confusion as a red Porsche screeched to a halt outside the house.

"Hello Lucy," drawled Tristan. "Ready are we?"

"Who's that old man?" whispered Amy to her mother.

"Shh darling," scolded Angela. "That's Tristan Proudfoot. He's a famous conductor and he conducts the choir Mummy and Lucy sing in."

Tristan gazed at Angela without recognition.

"You remember Angela, don't you Tristan?" stammered Lucy. "She's recently joined the choir."

"Oh yes," said Tristan blankly. Why would I remember a dumpy middle aged woman, he thought and yet perhaps I have seen her at choir. Her face looks a little familiar.

"Oh yes, of course I remember you. How are you enjoying my Belshazzar?"

"Your Belshazzar?" laughed Angela. "I thought it was William Walton's Belshazzar!"

Lucy smiled brightly. Why doesn't Angela go, she thought.

"Look Angela, I'll pop round on Monday after school and we can sort out a time for some note bashing. Is that

OK? Bye then. Yes, I'm ready, Tristan. I'll just lock the front door."

Why is Lucy interested in Tristan, wondered Angela as she led Amy back to No. 47.

"I want a piano lesson now! I want Lucy," whimpered Amy as Angela opened her front door.

"Oh Amy," laughed Angela. "You look like Pingu when you push your lips out like that. Come on, let's see who can do the best Pingu pout!"

"I won! I won!" shrieked Amy. "I'm Pingu! Pingu wants to play the piano!"

"All right, just one piece before bed, but not too loudly," said Angela. "We don't want to wake baby Claude now, do we?"

Baby Claude stirred in his sleep as Amy's Red Indian March pounded through the floor of his nursery. He put both hands up in front of him, like two little plump starfish, then his body relaxed and he drifted back to sleep, floating through a milky twilight.

Tristan's Porsche was roaring down the main road out of Springfield by this time, heading towards Kent.

"Where are we going?" asked a bewildered Lucy.

"Don't you worry sweetie," leered Tristan, "I'm taking you somewhere very special."

He patted her knee as the car accelerated.

"Have you heard of Castle Temple? No? It's a fabulous little village with one of the very best restaurants around. You'll adore it. Not long now."

"Doesn't your car go fast?" said Lucy admiringly. "Oh, look out! Oh, should you have stopped there for the lights?"

"There's no stopping me," said Tristan with a harsh laugh. "God, I'm dying for a cigarette. Mind if I smoke?"

"Well, actually," began Lucy.

"Oh, so you disapprove, do you?" laughed Tristan. "Tell me, what else do you disapprove of?"

"Mantovani and most early music, particularly long

slow pieces written for viols," replied Lucy, quick as a flash.

"A girl after my own heart," said Tristan softly. "I can see we're going to have a wonderful evening."

Lucy settled back into her seat happily. They drove through several villages, with Tristan taking no account of the signs to "Drive carefully," or "Respect our village."

"Bakesville," read Lucy and then thought to herself, Bakesville? Where have I heard that name? Bakesville? Oh, I know, Steve's parents live here, that's it. I wonder if he's arrived yet. He said he was spending the weekend here.

"Do you know Steve, Steve Goodman?" asked Lucy.

"No. Should I?" frowned Tristan. "Oh, wait a minute, he's a bass, isn't he? Oh yes, tall bloke, sits at the front sometimes. Good voice, you know. Very reliable. Well, what about him?"

"Oh nothing," replied Lucy "It's just that his parents live in Bakesville. I mean they live here and his mother's been really ill. She's had cancer."

"Really," said Tristan in a bored voice, inspecting his fingers as he was forced to stop at a red light. "How terrible. Weren't you having a drink with him on Wednesday? In the pub after choir?"

"Oh," blushed Lucy. "We were meant to go to the pub with a group, but no one else wanted to go. He's a nice man, you know."

"I expect he fancies you," growled Tristan. "I expect all the men at choir do. You are quite deliciously lovely you know, my sweet."

Tristan put his hand on Lucy's knee and Lucy didn't say anything else until they reached the restaurant in Castle Temple. "Here we are," drawled Tristan as he opened Lucy's car door. "What do you think of the place?"

Lucy stared up at the floodlit building with its impressive ivy clad walls.

"Castle Temple Hotel and Restaurant," she read. "Oh, it's fabulous," she exclaimed. "Just fabulous. Like something in a film."

"Glad you like it," said Tristan in a husky voice. "This way. Mind the step. Here, let me take your arm."

"Evening Mr Proudfoot," said a man in uniform. "Nice to see you again. Enjoy your evening."

"Oh! They know you! Have they seen you conducting?" asked Lucy.

"No sweetie," said Tristan with a barely suppressed smirk. "It's just that I've been here a few times before, many times in fact. It's a favourite haunt of mine."

"Somewhere to bring your ladies," said Lucy archly.

Tristan looked at her in surprise. Oh, I shouldn't have said that, thought Lucy. Why did I say that? What must he think of me? Oh, I've ruined the evening now!

"Well, yes," laughed Tristan. "I have brought a few ladies here in the past. My secret's out!"

Tristan took Lucy by the arm and steered her towards their table as he whispered in her ear,

"But none as lovely as you!"

"Oh Tristan," smiled Lucy, flattered, but she couldn't help feeling rather uncomfortable. What if it was all true, what everyone said about Tristan. Was he just a womaniser?

"Did you, have you, I mean, did you bring your wife here?" asked Lucy timidly.

"My wife?" snarled Tristan. "You mean my ex-wife, don't you?"

Lucy wanted to sink through the ground. Why did she keep saying the wrong thing?

"Well, yes," she stammered. "I'm so sorry. I meant to say your ex-wife. I'm so sorry Tristan. I really didn't mean to say that."

"Relax sweetie," said Tristan bitterly. "Forget it. Anyway, don't you mean ex-wives?" he added with a short bark of laughter. "I have been married twice after all. Don't seem to be very good at it!"

Oh Tristan, thought Lucy. You have been through so

much pain. I do so want to look after you. It will be fine when we are married. You'll see. Lucy was sensible enough not to say anything out loud to Tristan at this point.

"Would you like to order," enquired the waiter.

"A few more minutes," begged Tristan, who had put his sorrowful face on again. "But wait, you'd better bring us a drink."

He looks so tired, thought Lucy and his eyes are red. He probably doesn't look after himself. I hope I haven't upset him.

"Do you cook yourself proper meals at home?" Lucy asked Tristan.

Tristan stared at her in surprise.

"Are you interested in cooking," he said. "I wouldn't have thought it was your style."

"Well, I like cooking, but I'm not really very good at it. Not much experience I suppose," said Lucy, blushing.

"Do you blush all the time?" teased Tristan softly, reaching forward to stroke her cheek but Lucy moved backwards and studied the menu with great interest.

"The duck looks good," she commented, "or perhaps I'll try the veal. No, not veal; I can't bear to think of those little calves being slaughtered."

"Shall I choose for you?" asked Tristan. "I'm very good at choosing."

"No, it's all right," said Lucy. "I'll have the duck, thank you. What are you having?"

"Oh, some red meat," replied Tristan, licking his lips. "Definitely red meat of some sort. Dammit, where's that waiter got to with the wine? I'm dying for a drink."

You needn't think you can swear when we're married, thought Lucy primly.

Tristan caught sight of her face and laughed.

"Sorry sweetie! Forgot there was a lady present! It's just that I really need a drink."

Tristan loosened his collar, pulling at it with his fingers.

"Isn't it hot in here?" he asked. "Perhaps we shouldn't have sat so near the fire. Those logs give off a lot of heat!"

"But it's so pretty," exclaimed Lucy. "I love an open fire, don't you? When I have my own house, I'm going to have open fires in all the main rooms."

"That sounds romantic," drawled Tristan. "Ah, the wine at last! Here's to you, Lucy. Here's to the best looking girl in the room!"

Lucy stared round doubtfully at the other couples in the room. Most of the ladies were of the blue rinse brigade, but Lucy was sure that Tristan had meant to pay her a compliment.

"Thank you," smiled Lucy as their glasses clinked together. "Thank you for asking me out."

There was not much conversation during the first course as both Lucy and Tristan were intent on their food. Lucy was carefully trying to pick out all the fatty bits from the duck. She had forgotten how rich duck was and the chef seemed to have smothered the dish in a creamy sauce as well. She knew she couldn't stomach the whole thing, so she began stacking bits of duck fat under a piece of cabbage in what she hoped was an unobtrusive manner. The waiter stared at this procedure in fascination. Tristan didn't notice as he was tearing chunks from a large rare steak with his slightly pointed teeth and mopping up the blood and juices from his plate with hunks of bread.

"Mmm, delicious," he growled. "How's yours, Lucy?"

"Fine, thank you," she replied politely. "Full of flavour."

Secretly Lucy was wondering if Tristan had eaten anything at all today before this meal. He was devouring his steak so ferociously, it was rather like sitting opposite an animal at the kill.

"You seem to be enjoying the meat," Lucy ventured tentatively.

"Mmm," replied Tristan. "Can't talk, sorry, mouth full."

Meanwhile the staff in the restaurant kitchen were speculating as to whether Tristan would be booking a room for the night.

"He often does," observed the waiter.

"Ah yes," replied a pimply youth who was stirring some soup, "but the odd one gets away. Don't you remember the last time he was here, a few weeks ago? I think her name was Claire, a good looking girl she was, well, she slapped his face at the end of the meal and they didn't stay."

"I can just imagine what Tristan had suggested to her," leered the waiter. "He really is a one, that Tristan. Just can't settle for one woman, can he?"

Tristan too was thinking of the slap he had received last time he had been in the restaurant. He knew that no one else had noticed the incident and yet it had hurt his pride. Still, Claire had asked him round to her flat for a meal after that and despite a bit of a falling out, she had been very friendly at choir last Wednesday. Anyway, he wasn't going to make the same mistake with Lucy, oh no. He would take his time with this one. She seemed a bit on the timid side, although some of her comments had been pointed enough this evening.

"Dessert, madam?" the waiter asked Lucy.

"Oh no, I couldn't, no, really, thank you, just a coffee please."

"I'd better not either," said Tristan, patting his waistline and looking regretfully at the spotted dick and custard on a neighbouring table. "But doesn't that look delicious?"

Lucy stared at the pudding in horror.

"Think of the fat content," she said to Tristan sternly. "You're much better off with yoghurt or fruit."

"I don't think they serve yoghurt," said Tristan in surprise.

"We can provide yoghurt, if madam wishes," said the waiter in an oily voice.

"Oh no, that won't be necessary," laughed Lucy nervously. "Oh, just have what you want, Tristan; if you want spotted dick, have it!"

"I will then," leered Tristan. "I'll have exactly what I want!"

His hoarse laugh rang out in the restaurant in a disturbing way as he lit a cigarette.

"Just dying for one of these, absolutely dying," he said, taking a long slow drag.

Lucy pursed her lips, but wisely said nothing.

Tristan fell upon his pudding when it arrived.

"Can I tempt you to a mouthful?" he asked. "No? Here, let me hold the spoon for you."

"No thank you," said Lucy a little sharply. "Actually, I don't like puddings very much. I never seem to have room for them."

"Well, I hope you're not missing out just to watch your figure," said Tristan. "Leave me to watch that!"

Lucy felt uncomfortable with the way the conversation was going so she hastily drew her coffee cup up to her face, cradling it with both hands, elbows on the table, allowing the warmth of the coffee to steam over her nose and mouth.

"Mmm, wonderful coffee," she murmured, though privately she thought it too strong and bitter. In all honesty, she was as happy with a mug of instant decaf as anything, but she supposed Tristan, being a man of the world, would expect her to have more sophisticated tastes.

"I hope it doesn't keep me awake," she added.

"Don't you like being kept awake?" gurgled Tristan in a rather thick voice, his throat being full of custard at the time.

Oh really, thought Lucy crossly. Must he go on so? She was beginning to feel a little disappointed with the level of Tristan's wit, though perhaps he was worn out after studying musical scores all day and playing his piano. That's it, she thought. He must be exhausted, poor man.

Lucy regarded him tenderly but was surprised to find that another feeling was creeping over her. The feeling had been there for some time, but she was only just beginning to notice its slow invasion.

"Another coffee?" asked Tristan. "No? How about a nightcap? Go on! I'm going to."

That's it, thought Lucy. I know that feeling. It's boredom. I'm bored. How terribly ungrateful of me, after Tristan has gone to all this trouble. Perhaps I'm overtired too. Perhaps it's my job. That's it, my job is taking away all my sense of fun. But I do wish Tristan would stop making suggestive remarks and actually talk to me. I didn't expect him to be like this.

"No, no nightcap, thank you," said Lucy. "Honestly, I've had a lovely evening and I don't drink much anyway."

"Good for you," smiled Tristan. "I tell you what, I'll pass on the nightcap too. What do you say to a little stroll in the garden before we head back? Waiter, the bill please."

"The garden?" asked Lucy, startled. "But it's night time."

"Very observant of you," said Tristan dryly, "but the garden is floodlit. It is such a lovely garden, it seems a shame to leave without seeing it and you can see the stars properly out here in the countryside, you know; it's not like in the town."

"The stars!" cried Lucy. "Oh, how romantic! Yes, let's go and look at the stars!"

"Steady on Lucy!" laughed Tristan as he bent over to sign his credit card slip. "You don't want everyone following us, do you?"

"No I suppose not," replied Lucy. "Oh! Goodness me!"

"What is it" asked Tristan, raising his head slightly.

"Oh, nothing," gasped Lucy. She couldn't possibly tell him that she had just noticed his bald patch in all its glory. She knew that his hair was thinning a little, that was only natural, male hormones, she knew all about that. What

Lucy hadn't suspected was that Tristan had been combing great long strands of his hair over the crown of his head. When he had leaned forward, this hair had fallen away to reveal a large bald patch in a most unbecoming way. Really, this wouldn't do at all, thought Lucy to herself. Men should admit their baldness and keep their hair short on the top. She would sort this out for Tristan; she just needed the right moment to tell him. Luckily, Lucy knew instinctively that this was not the right moment.

"Nothing's wrong," smiled Lucy. "Just making a few plans, that's all."

"Well, I hope they include me," teased Tristan.

"I couldn't possibly say," replied Lucy archly.

"Does sir require anything else?" asked the oily waiter.

"No thank you," said Tristan as he led Lucy out of the dining room and into the garden, pausing only to look regretfully at the wide curved staircase that led from the entrance hall up to the hotel bedrooms.

"Another time," he murmured to himself. "Another time."

The garden was not as light as Tristan had said and they both stumbled across the wet grass in some confusion.

"I know the path is somewhere around here," grumbled Tristan. "I suppose they're saving money, not lighting the garden."

"Well, it is the middle of the winter," observed Lucy, a little sourly Tristan thought. "Where is this path then?"

Lucy felt annoyed as her heels sank into a patch of mud. Bother, she thought. Suede is so difficult to clean.

"Here it is," cried Tristan at last, after breaking through a sort of scratchy hedge. "Can you squeeze through this? Here, let me hold your arm."

"I'm all right," said Lucy in a cross voice. "No, really, I can manage." At last, she thought, I can stand on a patch of dry land. I'm sure I've pulled a thread in my trousers.

Lucy looked around her and saw that they were both

standing on a tiny path leading up to a stone urn which presumably became a fountain in the summer months. Four equal paths ran from the urn, each covered by an arched walk.

"Roses," said Lucy. "That's why it's so scratchy. It must be a picture in the summer."

"Look," whispered Tristan in sudden awe. "Millions and millions of them. Just look at them twinkling up there."

They gazed up at the stars and felt that familiar sense of both their own insignificance and the wonder of the universe.

Everything will be all right, thought Lucy. Whatever happens, all will be well. I do hope Steve's mum is getting better. It's so cruel when illness strikes. Oh, I do feel sorry for Steve. Lucy remembered her own father's sudden death and tears came to her eyes.

Steady, thought Tristan, steady, I mustn't rush her. He put his arms gently around Lucy and she tilted her head to look up at him. Steve, she thought, Steve is so brave. I wonder what he's doing now. When Tristan kissed her with his usual practised ease, she felt nothing except a slight distaste for the alcohol and cigarettes on his breath. I thought I wanted this, she said to herself. I thought I knew what I wanted.

Lucy buried her face in Tristan's jacket and began to cry.

"What's wrong, sweetie," Tristan asked with sudden concern. "Has someone treated you badly? Just let me get my hands on him, I'll..."

"No," sobbed Lucy. "There's nothing wrong, oh, it's just I feel all mixed up, you know, seeing the stars like that and then I thought of my dad and anyone who's been ill, oh, it's all too much."

"Well, dry your eyes," said Tristan, trying hard not to sound exasperated. Women, he thought. They just don't know what they want. He handed her a large white crumpled handkerchief. "Here, dry your eyes. Perhaps we'd better be getting back."

Tristan gave Lucy a hug, patting her back in an absent minded way. Looking over Tristan's shoulder, Lucy could see in the distance, through an arched hedge, a grey and mossy statue of a young water nymph standing on a raised plinth with a water pitcher at her feet and several large branches from nearby shrubs growing over her. The nymph was rather unsuccessfully trying to hold her drapery over her body to preserve her modesty.

"There, there," said Tristan. "Let's make our way back to the car. Mind where you step!"

The water nymph looked coyly at Tristan and Lucy as they felt their way down the path.

"I'd better take you home, sweetie," whispered Tristan. "Not that you need your beauty sleep, but perhaps I do."

"I am rather tired," admitted Lucy. "It's been a long week."

Lucy felt Tristan's rather grubby handkerchief in her pocket. Should I offer it back to him, she wondered, or should I wash it first? What is the correct etiquette with handkerchiefs lent to damsels in distress? Lucy gave a giggle as she began penning in her mind the letter she might write to a magazine on the subject.

"Dear Miss Manners,

What is the correct etiquette when one's young, no, possibly one's mature swain has lent one a grubby handkerchief…"

"Feeling better?" asked Tristan.

"Yes, thank you," replied Lucy gratefully. "And thanks for a lovely evening. Sorry if I ruined it for you by being pathetic."

God, she's lovely, thought Tristan as he helped Lucy into the car. And yet… and yet… He didn't know what he really felt. Certainly, Lucy had behaved in a way that had surprised him once or twice during the evening. She was no pushover, that was for sure, but Tristan wasn't really sure he wanted her to be. It's not only women who don't know what they want, he thought to himself as he accelerated down the gravel drive and joined the main road with scarcely a glance to left or right.

The journey back seemed even shorter than the journey there. They sped through empty lanes and roads, with the speedometer of the Porsche reading mostly well over 80mph.

Lucy remembered that she wanted to ask Tristan to the party at Grangewood Golf Club but she didn't quite know how to frame the invitation.

"Would you, could you. . ." she began.

"What?" said Tristan, turning to look at her.

"Oh, keep your eyes on the road!" gasped Lucy as they sped along the dark winding lanes.

"Would you like to go to a party, I mean, with me? It's a sort of end of term Christmas thing, it's at Grangewood Golf Club and it's for the staff, plus friends and family of Springfield High School and Fairfield High School."

"Will it be fun?" leered Tristan. "Is there music?"

"Oh, you'd love the band," said Lucy. "It's the Blue Sunset Band. Do you know them?"

"Know them? I used to play for them," shouted Tristan with a bark of laughter. Oh yes, great, I'll come. I played with them when they first started for about two years I think, then I got busy doing other things, anyway, I don't suppose any of the original band are left now, probably a bunch of youngsters, but it was great fun."

Tristan's face took on a wistful look as he remembered his sessions with the band. He had still been married then, to his first wife that is and she hadn't been keen on him spending all those evenings rehearsing, but what the hell, he had carried on anyway. Carried on until they had found another pianist. Something about "fitting in better" they had said to him. It was a shame, because he'd enjoyed it, but he was getting so busy with other work that he didn't have enough time for the band. He had been going places then, really going places. Winning that big conducting competition had helped and then the offer to teach at the Royal College of Music had come in. Pity that hadn't worked out, but he just couldn't be available for all those commitments during term time, didn't see why he should be. And then his marriage had started to go wrong and the drinking had started. . .

Lucy looked at Tristan and noticed his faraway expression. He must be reminiscing about his days with the Blue Sunset Band, she thought fondly; he must be remembering all those rehearsal sessions and concerts.

"What was your favourite number?" asked Lucy.

"My what?" asked Tristan, startled.

"You know, your favourite piece that you played with the band all those years ago," persisted Lucy.

"I, I can't remember," replied Tristan sadly. "And it wasn't that long ago. Was it? Look, Lucy, I think you've got the wrong idea about me, I mean, what I'm trying to say is, you don't know what I'm like, do you? Not really?"

"Well, I'm trying to find out," Lucy replied with a smile.

Oh hell, thought Tristan, this isn't working out the way it should at all. Why can't I just be my normal self with her?

There was no more conversation in the car until they reached the outskirts of Springfield and Tristan sensibly slowed down a little.

"Where do you live?" he asked. "Which road?"

"Don't you know?" asked Lucy. "How did you, I mean, I thought you must know because of the flowers. It's not this way, take the next right, that's it; it's Stanhope Gardens. Do you know it?"

"Stanhope Gardens? I've seen the name. Let me think, oh, yes," Tristan said with a chuckle. "I remember."

He had remembered that Claire's flat was near and that he had driven down Stanhope Gardens on his way home from having lunch with her last Sunday.

"And what's this about flowers?" asked Tristan.

"I, I thought you'd sent me flowers," said Lucy awkwardly. "I did ask you on the phone."

Tristan coloured slightly as he recalled the conversation and how he had let Lucy go on believing that he had sent the flowers.

"Well, I should have sent you flowers," he said gallantly. "And now I know your address I can," he added, patting her on the knee as they pulled up outside Lucy's flat.

"I'll see you at choir next week, won't I?" asked Lucy. "I'm going away for the weekend tomorrow morning, quite early. I'm going to stay with my sister Caroline in Bath, you know I mentioned her before, just for the weekend."

"Oh really," commented Tristan in a rather bored voice. Just as well Lucy will be away, Tristan thought, because I might pay Claire a visit this weekend and Lucy's flat is a little too close to Claire's for comfort.

"Stay there; I'll come round and open your door."

Tristan levered himself out of his car with a grunt. Why are cars like this so low, he wondered. Still, they look good and that's the main thing.

"Here you are, sweetie," he said to Lucy as he helped her out. "Your bed awaits you," he added with a wink.

"Oh Tristan," laughed Lucy. "You are terrible!" She gave him a quick peck on the cheek, then ran towards her front door, surprised at her own boldness. "Don't forget you promised to come to the party at Grangewood Golf Club," she called softly. "It's a week on Saturday. Put it in your diary."

"How could I forget," smiled Tristan.

"Thank you for a lovely evening," Lucy added.

"The first of many," smirked Tristan as he folded himself back in his car. He waited until Lucy had let herself into her house then drove off noisily into the night.

Angela peered out of her bedroom window, woken by the noise of the car doors.

"Come back to bed," whispered her husband, Jeffrey, sleepily.

Angela climbed back into bed, grateful as ever that she had found Jeffrey and no longer had to go through the roller coaster of emotions that Lucy was facing.

"I hope she knows what she's doing," Angela began, but Jeffrey had already turned over and begun to snore gently.

Tristan wondered for a fleeting moment whether it was worth driving round to Claire's flat to see if she was still up. No, he thought with an angry clash of gears; better get home.

He felt vaguely uneasy as he drove along the deserted main roads through Springfield to reach his home. Pausing briefly at a red light, he suddenly realised what was niggling away at him. If he hadn't sent Lucy flowers, who had?

"Damn!" he shouted. "Damn and blast!"

He had tried to behave like a gentleman this evening, but perhaps he should have come on a bit more strongly. No, he thought sadly, that wouldn't have worked. Maybe he was losing his touch and yet Lucy seemed very keen on him, almost hero worshipped him, put him on a pedestal. I could so easily disappoint her, he thought.

"Pull yourself together!" Tristan shouted to the empty car interior. "Tristan Proudfoot disappoint a woman? The idea is absurd!" And with that, Tristan sped home, his head full of strategic plans for the hunt.

Lucy noticed the fresh smell of the flowers as soon as she let herself into the flat. She flopped onto the sofa next to the vase and reached out to touch the flowers carefully with her fingertips. She could feel the soft freshness of the blooms as her fingers moved gently over them and then she felt the rougher texture of the greenery. Julia was still out, although it was after midnight. Lucy sighed happily, going over the events of the evening in her mind but frowning slightly as she remembered the scene in the garden. She was disappointed too that Tristan hadn't sent her the flowers but not as disappointed as she had thought she would be. More embarrassed, if anything, that she had just assumed that it had been Tristan.

"And how shabby of him to let me think that," said Lucy aloud. "But who are the flowers from?"

The question echoed round the sitting room and looking into her heart, Lucy realised that she knew and had known for some time.

"Why, it's Steve, of course, Steve. He's the one."

Chapter Six: A great city

Lucy woke early the next morning, looking forward to her weekend in Bath with her sister Caroline and her family. She sprang out of bed and took a quick peek out of the window. The sky was bright and clear and Lucy could see frost glinting on the grass in the back garden. She opened the window and smelt the cold crisp air. There was scarcely any sound of traffic this Saturday morning, just the distant electric whine of the milk float and the chinking of milk bottles. I must hurry, thought Lucy. I've got to get up to Waterloo, across London and then to Paddington by 9 o'clock to catch the Bath train. She showered and dressed hurriedly, tiptoeing past Julia's room as she knew that her flatmate rarely surfaced at the weekend before 11 am. Lucy picked up the overnight bag that she had packed carefully the night before and slipped out of the house, making her way to Springfield Station to catch the train to Waterloo.

At almost the same time, Steve was beginning his journey by car to Bakesville, to spend the weekend with his parents. He had slept badly following a phone call from his father the previous night.

"What is it Dad?" he had asked. "Everything's OK isn't it? Is there a change of plan?"

"Look Steve," said his father. "I don't want you to worry and I don't want to upset you. I suppose I should tell you tomorrow, it's just that, I don't know what to say really, it's nothing special you know."

"Dad, what is it?" Steve had said gently. "You can tell me; I'm not a child any more you know."

"Of course," replied his father. "You've been wonderful and you should know, you've a right to know, it's just that I'm so worried about your mother. She hasn't eaten all day, doesn't feel like it, she says. It's as if she's given up."

"Have you rung the doctor?" asked Steve, thoroughly alarmed by now.

"Well, I did ring this morning and he said not to worry, let her rest and he'd pop in on Saturday morning to see her, but obviously if she becomes much worse I can call him again. It's just that I feel it's different this time; I know we've had these scares before and she's always pulled through but it's really got to me this time. I won't be able to face life without her, you know."

Steve chatted to his father for a long time, reassuring him the best he could.

"Now Dad, go and see how Mum is. Maybe she'd like a bit of that soup in the freezer? You know, the one in the cardboard carton. There's plenty in the freezer; I put it in there myself last weekend. You can heat it in the microwave. Anyway, you should eat too, shouldn't you? I'll see you tomorrow, as early as I can; now try not to worry."

Steve had put the phone down with a heavy heart and tried to finish his work without much success. On Saturday morning, after a fitful night's sleep, he snatched a quick coffee and a bowl of cereal, then began the journey to his parents' house, fearful of what awaited him.

Lucy got to Waterloo very quickly, then battled her way to Paddington on the tube, getting incredibly hot and crushed. Why is the tube always crowded, she wondered. Where is everyone going? She stared with interest at the other occupants of her carriage. There was a mother with two girls with their hair pinned neatly up. Probably going to dancing lessons, decided Lucy. Then she noticed a woman in her early twenties with heavy eye make up and a shiny black dress on. Probably not been home yet, thought Lucy with a giggle. Next to the young woman, there was a man in a business suit looking worried and glancing at his watch. Possibly making his way to Heathrow, speculated Lucy, but he's rather late. Oh poor thing, I hope he makes it in time. She smiled sympathetically at the business man, who then leered at her in a rather disconcerting fashion. Lucy looked away, feeling thoroughly uncomfortable and fished a paperback out of her bag, to hide her confusion. That will teach me to mind my own business, she thought wryly.

She reached Paddington with plenty of time to spare, so she treated herself to a cappuccino and a fresh croissant. Delicious, thought Lucy happily. I could live on this. She remembered all the rich food from the night before and blushed as she thought of Tristan kissing her. Then she imagined what it would be like if Steve kissed her. Heavens, she thought, what am I turning into?

Lucy elbowed her way into WH Smith to buy a magazine to read on the journey.

"What to do if you love two men at once," screamed a bold headline.

"How to have the perfect Christmas."

"How to protect your skin this winter."

"Bin the clutter and reorganise your life."

Nice idea, thought Lucy, but impractical. There will always be clutter in my life and I sort of enjoy it really. It makes life more interesting.

"Oh sorry," Lucy apologised as she bumped into the two girls with the pinned back hair from the tube. They were also eagerly scanning the magazines and giggling.

"Sorry, didn't mean to push."

"That's all right," said one of the girls brightly. "It's so crowded, isn't it? You were in the tube, weren't you?"

"Yes," smiled Lucy. "I noticed you too."

"You should buy that magazine," advised the other girl, pointing to the magazine that Lucy was holding. "My mum, she says that one's really good; lots of stuff on the menopause and she got some very comfy shoes from an advert in the back, too."

The first girl nodded wisely.

"Perhaps not," snapped Lucy starchily. "I think this one about wanting two lovers is more my sort of thing."

The two girls gaped at her as she positively ran to the till with her magazine.

"Who would have thought it?" remarked one of the girls and the other shook her head in a world weary fashion.

Thus it was that Lucy found herself on the train reading an article about having two men in your life at once.

"It is not usually the case," the article asserted, "that a woman can actually be in love with two men at once. She only thinks she is. One man will be her true love, the other probably an obsession, a crush or a mistake. This could be a sign of immaturity…"

Lucy wriggled uncomfortably in her seat.

"The woman must look into her heart and see what she really wants. Is she looking for a lasting relationship, marriage and children possibly, or is she after a one night stand or a fling?"

What utter tosh, thought Lucy angrily.

"Sometimes," the article continued piously, "sometimes the woman is attracted to an older man because of a troubled family background. Counselling can help in extreme cases…"

I think I'd prefer to read about a perfect Christmas, thought Lucy, flicking the pages furiously. Oh, great, ideas for presents. Perhaps I should buy presents for Caroline, Jeremy and the twins when I'm down in Bath, then I could leave them there, all wrapped up and ready for Christmas. Oh, I do love Christmas, thought Lucy happily. All those lights and sparkly things and yummy things to eat. Oh good, some ideas for presents for children. I'm sure Rebecca and Teresa would like something here and of course the shops are great in Bath. I could go shopping this afternoon, just nip out for an hour. Lucy settled down happily to read as the countryside sped past her.

Meanwhile Steve had long since arrived at his parents'

house. He had been shocked at his mother's appearance and had felt quite desperate when he had cradled her in his arms.

"Hello Mum," he had sighed, fighting back the tears. "How are you feeling? I hear you're not eating; you really must you know."

"Oh I'm all right Steve," she had replied "Just so tired. I think I'll go and have another rest."

Later, Steve and his father sat chatting over a cup of coffee, waiting for the doctor to come.

"I'm sure this is the end," said Steve's father gloomily. "She's giving up; I know she is."

"You don't know anything of the sort," said Steve, putting his hand over his father's. "You're so tired, you can't think straight. Let's see what the doctor has to say."

"I'm so pleased you're here," said Steve's father. "You make all the difference you know. And how's that job of yours going? Taught anything useful yet?"

"It depends how useful you think learning about the Industrial Revolution is," replied Steve, with an attempt at a laugh that didn't come out quite right.

When the doctor arrived, he was very positive.

"I did warn you that she might lose her appetite for a bit, do you remember?"

"But doctor, she's so drained and her spirits are so low."

"Depression is very common in these cases." replied the doctor. "Let's see if we can continue as we are for a bit longer. Just give her a chance to settle down, after all, she's had a big operation only a few months ago and I don't want to put her on medication for depression if it's not necessary."

"She certainly won't want to take any more pills," fretted Steve's father. "But is there really an alternative? How can we help her?"

"She needs lots of support," continued the doctor, "not that she's not getting it from both of you," he added hastily, after a quick look at Steve's face. "Perhaps one of your sisters could come and stay, Steve? Women are so good in this sort of situation."

And with that he was gone.

"The man's a fool," said Steve's father scornfully. "An absolute fool. He hasn't got a clue."

"He's doing his best," said Steve. "And actually I think he was quite reassuring. Things aren't as bleak as you think, Dad and it's not such a bad idea to have someone else staying. You could do with a break."

"But your sisters are both so busy," said Steve's dad. "Charlotte said she'd pop in tomorrow but she can't stay because of the children and Emma's got to be careful now that she's expecting."

"Is she? Emma's having a baby? How wonderful," said Steve in delighted surprise.

"Oh, me and my big mouth!" said his father. "She only told us yesterday and she wants to tell you herself. Try to sound surprised, won't you?"

"Sure," laughed Steve. "Some good news at last. That's brilliant! And I thought they'd never get round to it, Emma and that husband of hers. They both seemed so busy with their careers. Anyway Dad, I didn't mean that one of the girls should stay; I meant that I could move in for a time."

"You?" his father said in surprise. "But what about your job?"

"I can easily commute to work from here," answered Steve. "OK, it will mean an early start because of the traffic, but at least I can be here in the evenings for you, make sure you both have a decent meal and do what I can; after all Dad, I don't want you getting ill from all the extra work."

"And when would you relax or get a decent night's sleep?" demanded his father. "I know you; you'd be up until all hours with your school work then have to leave at the crack of dawn to get to school on time. No, it just wouldn't work. I forbid it."

"I can be stubborn too," grinned Steve. "And I say that I'm going to give it a try. Besides, how much relaxation and sleep do you think I've been getting, worrying about you and Mum? I might as well be here worrying and doing something useful rather than worrying on my own in my flat."

"All right, I give in," smiled Steve's father. "I have to admit it's all getting a bit much for me. But one thing I insist on; you must still go to your choir rehearsals. I know how much you enjoy them and we've got tickets for your concert. Your mother is very keen to go."

"It's a deal," said Steve.

"Anyway," continued his father, "aren't you quite keen on a certain young lady in the choir? I thought so! Lucy, isn't it?"

"Yes, Lucy," replied Steve, looking embarrassed. "Yes, I'm keen, more keen than she is, I think. She's keen on someone else; not sure how serious that is."

"Courage!" shouted Steve's father. "Faint heart never won fair lady! I presume she is fair? And a lady?"

"Definitely," grinned Steve. "Thanks Dad, you've cheered me up. She's worth a fight, is Lucy. She's the tops."

"Who's the tops?" asked Steve's mother, coming out of the kitchen. "Have you got a young lady, Steve?"

"Oh Mum," said Steve, suddenly uncomfortable.

"You can ask her here anytime, you know." continued his mother. "We'd like to meet her, wouldn't we David?"

"It's not reached that stage yet," said Steve. "But Mum, you look so much better. You had me quite worried when I first arrived."

"Sorry darling. There's no need to worry. I'm only tired. I haven't recovered from the operation yet. It takes ages, you know. Now, what's for lunch? I'm feeling a bit peckish." And with that, she wandered back to the sitting room.

Steve and his father looked at each other, mightily relieved.

"This is what it's like, son. Up one minute, down the next. This is what you're letting yourself in for."

"I can cope, Dad; I'm going to look after you both," replied Steve, putting his arm round his father. "You're to stop worrying. Mum's going to be fine. It's bound to take time. You'll see."

Steve hummed to himself as he prepared a light lunch for the three of them. His worst fears had not been confirmed and yet he knew they still had a long way to go with his mother's illness. Things could still go either way for her and at the very least, she had a long road to recovery ahead of her. Perhaps I should let my flat, wondered Steve and move in for six months or so? But no, I can't make decisions like that yet. Better take it a day at a time. Mum's priority now is lots of rest and good food, Dad's too really. I'd better brush up my cooking skills; I wonder if Lucy knows much about cooking? I could ask her advice as my sisters are so busy.

Steve's thoughts were interrupted by the telephone ringing. It was his sister, Emma.

"No Emma, nothing to worry about; they need a bit of looking after, that's all," Steve told his sister. "You are? Early next summer? A summer baby? Oh, how marvellous! Yes, of course I'm surprised! What great news! Congratulations to you both!"

What with Charlotte's two children and now Emma's baby, I'm going to be a very busy uncle, thought Steve as he put the phone down with a smile. He began to wonder how Lucy was getting on down in the West Country with her two nieces. Funny there being twins in her family as well.

"I bet she's a smashing auntie," said Steve out loud.

"Did you say something, dear," called Steve's mother from the next room.

"Oh no," said Steve. "Talking to myself, as usual.

Lunch is ready; are you happy to eat now?"

"I'm happy you're here, my darling," said Steve's mother, coming into the kitchen. "Your visits mean so much to us."

"Oh Mum," whispered Steve and he held her slight frame close to him, worried again as he realised how thin and fragile she had become.

"Mum, you get better now, do you hear? That's the only thing we want. You take care. Now, sit down here and tell me what you think of this omelette. Dad! Are you coming? It's lunch time!"

Lucy was also sitting down to lunch, in the middle of Caroline's large, untidy but undoubtedly stylish kitchen. Rebecca and Teresa were sitting one either side of their aunt, looking very excited.

"You will come with us when Mummy takes us to ballet, won't you Aunty Lucy?"

"Yes, you know we have our ballet class, don't you? It's at two o'clock. That's why we're having lunch a bit early, so we can digest our food."

"And I'm going to wear a green tutu."

"Well, mine's yellow."

"I wanted yellow."

"Well, I wanted green."

"If you wanted green, then I want green too."

"But you've got the green one," interrupted Caroline despairingly. "Honestly Lucy, if you give them the same colour, they don't like it, but give them different colours and they only want what the other one has, or in this case what the other one hasn't got, but would have if I'd let her choose."

"I think I can follow that," laughed Lucy. "I'm sure we would have been just the same if we'd been closer in age."

"Lucky for Mum that there was such a gap between us," remarked Caroline as she got up from her chair. "Oops, I forgot this! Anyone want some salad?"

Caroline plonked a large shallow bowl on the table, brimming over with delicious looking lettuces and herbs.

"Serving up designer leaves again I see, my darling," said Jeremy appreciatively. "And this quiche is fabulous! One of your best."

"It's the free range organic eggs that make it taste so good," said Caroline smugly. "That and the fact that I use Gruyère cheese, not mouse trap like most people."

"What about the pastry, Caroline," asked Lucy. "I never seem to be able to do pastry properly."

"Well…" began Caroline.

"Mummy buys the pastry packets and keeps them in the freezer," chimed in Teresa.

"Yes," said Rebecca, "and she lets us make things out of the funny bits left over. We've made some today. You can eat them later!"

"I've been caught out," confessed Caroline with a blush. "Everyone has to cut some corners and who's got time to make their own pastry every time? Certainly not me."

"I sincerely hope it was organic frozen ready-made pastry," quipped Jeremy.

"Would you like a piece of french bread thrown at you?" demanded Caroline.

"Only if it's 100% organic wholemeal," replied Jeremy.

"Now that would hurt," laughed Caroline. "It would be like having a brick thrown at you."

I hope I can have a laugh with my husband when I get married, thought Lucy wistfully. Caroline and Jeremy seem to be getting on really well, much better than when the twins were tiny and Caroline was always so tired and over bearing. Jeremy knows how to make her laugh and he absolutely adores her. I wonder if I'll ever marry and have a family, or ever be adored by a lovely man, Lucy pondered as her eyes grew vague and tearful.

"Do you, Aunty Lucy?" demanded Rebecca. "Well, do you?"

"Do I what?" asked Lucy, alarmed at being dragged back to reality so suddenly.

"Do you want ice cream? Because we do."

"Yes, we do."

"We want, what colour do we want, Teresa?"

"We want pink," said Teresa firmly.

"Yes, pink." said Rebecca.

"You'll get what I've got," laughed Caroline. "Now, let's see, strawberry ice cream. . . where is it?"

Lucy stared at her sister's figure in fascinated horror as Caroline bent right into the chest freezer to retrieve the pink ice cream. The effect was that of an out of condition hippo struggling to bend over, hampered by multiple rolls of flab.

"I don't think I'll have any ice cream thanks," said Lucy hastily. "I'm happy with an apple."

"Got it," shouted Caroline in triumph. "Got it at last! Hiding at the bottom of the freezer it was!"

She held the tub aloft for all to admire.

"Not that one! Yuk!" yelled Teresa.

"Yucky," commented Rebecca. "It's got lumps in."

"They're strawberries," said an exasperated Caroline.

"We don't like strawberries," said Teresa. "They're yucky."

"But that's why the ice cream's pink, isn't it?" asked Lucy. "Because it's got strawberries in? Or have I missed something?"

"You haven't missed anything," laughed Jeremy. "It's just that these two little monsters, despite all our efforts, actually prefer the totally synthetic and guaranteed lump free ice cream that you can buy in the supermarkets."

"Frozen, coloured pig fat," commented Caroline. "That's what that stuff is, you know. Some of it actually boasts that it's a "non dairy product", as if that's something to be proud of! Ice cream should be just that, frozen cream with eggs and sugar too, of course and strawberries if it's pink. Anyway," Caroline continued, glaring at her sulky offspring, "This is what you're getting. Something decent! No doubt you'll get plenty of the other sort of ice cream at your friends' houses and at school."

"Jemima's mum always buys that lovely square stuff," bleated Rebecca.

"Square ice cream?" asked Lucy in amazement.

"Yes," explained Teresa, "all different squares, pink and yellow and brown. We love that."

"Oh," laughed Lucy, "You mean Neapolitan ice cream! Why, I remember having that when I was little. Do you remember Mum buying that, Caroline?"

"Oh I'm sure we were fed all sorts of rubbish when we were growing up," said Caroline contemptuously. "But people know better now. Well, girls, it's this ice cream or nothing. Come on, what's it to be?"

"That will do," said Rebecca sulkily.

"OK Mum," beamed Teresa. "In fact, I quite like it Mum! It's Rebecca that doesn't, you know. I like healthy food, like you do."

"Stop sucking up to your mother, Teresa," was Jeremy's only comment and that put an end to the talking about ice cream as the children and Caroline began tucking into great platefuls of it.

"Sure you're OK with a Braeburn, Lucy? You too, Jeremy?"

"Fine thanks," said Lucy through delicious mouthfuls of crisp juicy apple. "You know I'm not all that keen on ice cream; it's so cold!"

Rebecca and Teresa gazed at their aunt in astonishment. They didn't know anyone else who thought ice cream was too cold. Could their Aunty Lucy be ill, they wondered? Really, grown ups were very odd sometimes.

After lunch, Caroline, Lucy and the twins set off to the "Doyle Academy of Dancing".

"Have you got your bag, Rebecca?" asked Caroline. "You too, Teresa? I put the bags ready with your leotards, shoes and tights."

"But Mummy, we told you we had to wear tutus as well this week. It is a dress rehearsal, Mrs Doyle said. That means you have to wear a tutu."

"As opposed to a dress, I suppose," laughed Caroline. "Don't worry, I put the tutus in as well. Come on then, off we go, singing and dancing."

The twins skipped their way to Caroline's rather battered and ancient car.

"I want to sit next to Aunty Lucy!"

"No! I do. It's my turn!"

"Lucy's sitting in the front with me," said Caroline firmly. "That's enough of that nonsense. Now come on, get in. OK Lucy? Let's go then."

"Belt up! Belt up!" shouted Teresa.

"Yes, belt up, Mummy! Oh belt up!"

"That's enough of that," said Caroline, secretly amused. "You see," she explained to Lucy in a whisper, "the only time I let them say "belt up" to anyone is when we're in the car."

Lucy looked at her sister with incomprehension.

"Belt up!" shouted Caroline. "You know, seat belt! Put your seat belt on!"

"Oh," said Lucy and then laughed politely.

"I know, I know," apologised Caroline, shaking her head. "My sense of humour has gone to pot since having the kids!"

They were soon at the dancing school which was situated in a wide quiet street on the other side of Bath. "Doyle's Academy of Dancing" had deep stone steps leading up to a battered white front door with a large brass handle. Gaggles of giggling girls were flitting up the steps with their pink ballet bags flying behind them. Their hair was scrapped back into buns and festooned with hair grips and slides to hold awkward curls. Rebecca and Teresa both patted their heads smugly, convinced of the superiority of their own coiffures. Their Aunty Lucy had helped them put their hair up before lunch and had even allowed them a little touch of hairspray to hold it all in place. Really, Aunty Lucy was so much better at doing hair than their mother and they both wished that Lucy could come and live with them. She would be so useful, like having a maid in the house.

"Will you live with us, Aunty Lucy?" demanded Rebecca. "For ever?"

"Yes, for ever and ever," echoed Teresa.

"What a sweet thought girls," gushed Caroline, "But your Aunty Lucy is far too busy with her own life to live with us, but of course she can come and stay whenever she wants. You'll stay for Christmas, won't you, Lucy?" Caroline asked her sister. "Jeremy and I would love it if you would."

"I'm not sure yet," said Lucy. "It's so kind of you but I did sort of wonder about going out to France, to stay with Mum."

"No point," said Caroline. "She's coming to stay with us. Didn't you know?"

"Mum," came a whine from the back of the car. "Are we ever going in? We'll be late."

"Oh heavens," shrieked Caroline "Just listen to me bumbling on. Let's go kids. Do you want to come in for a few minutes, Lucy, to see Mrs Doyle? I don't suppose the place has changed at all since you came here all those years ago. Mrs Doyle is still exactly the same, just a few more lines!"

"I'd love to come in," smiled Lucy. As she ran up the steps of the Doyle Academy, hand in hand with Rebecca and Teresa, Lucy felt the years roll back. She had been one of those giggling excited girls rushing in to be drilled by the fearsome Mrs Doyle in all manner of complicated dance steps.

"Feet out! Derrières in! Do your best gels!"

Lucy could still hear the commands echoing in her mind. Turning her feet out a little and sucking her tummy in, Lucy walked into the studio to say "hello" to her old ballet teacher.

Mrs Doyle was posing at the barre in front of a full length mirror. She was a bizarre sight, with her grey hair held back by a pink nylon hair band and her feet turned out at right angles in large scuffed ballet shoes. Her face betrayed an over hasty application of make up, with a lopsided scarlet mouth, generously powdered nose and one eyebrow pencilled in a little higher than the other. She dabbed at her nose with a tiny lace hankerchief and then boomed out,

"Now come along gels! We haven't got all day! Get changed quickly! Into your leotards quickly! No, not the tutus yet, Hermione. We'll try those on later. Leotards first and cardigans if you're cold. Take your positions at the barre quickly - you know it's the show tomorrow afternoon. Why, it's Lucy! Lucy my darling! Come here my child."

Audrey Doyle swooped over to Lucy and gathered her favourite ex-pupil into her arms, leaving traces of powder and lipstick on Lucy's shoulders and cheeks.

"Are you coming to our show? Our show tomorrow?" Mrs Doyle demanded.

"Why, yes Mrs Doyle, I mean Audrey," answered Lucy. "I wouldn't miss it for the world."

"Wonderful! Joyous rapture!" trilled Mrs Doyle. "I'll see you then; must start the rehearsal you know! Things to do, girls to train! No rest for the wicked! Do stay and watch for a few minutes; you're very welcome, Lucy my darling."

"Why, thank you," said a blushing Lucy. "Yes, I will stay for a little while, if you're sure you don't mind?"

"Mind?" shrieked Audrey Doyle. "It's my pleasure, darling!" And with that, Mrs Doyle pirouetted across the floor to her pupils.

"Girls! Now come on girls! Let's get to work!"

"I think I'll stay for a bit," Lucy whispered to her sister

Caroline, "and then I'll do a bit of Christmas shopping and make my own way home as we arranged."

"Fine," answered Caroline. "You have a good time! I'm dashing to Sainsbury's – just got time to do a decent shop before I pick the little monsters up again to take them home. Now don't spend all your money on presents, Lucy. Buy something for yourself. You could do with a bit of pampering!"

With that advice, Caroline was gone and Lucy settled down at the back of the room to watch some of the rehearsal.

"Take your positions at the barre!" boomed out Mrs Doyle's voice. "Derrière in Hermione! Oh dear! You'd better not walk like that tomorrow!"

A troop of giggling, excited girls streamed across the room to their places, ballet shoes tapping softly on the wooden floor. The room was lit up with the pale blues and the sugar pinks of their leotards and cross over cardigans; each girl was going to do her very best this afternoon. As the music started, Lucy looked around the rehearsal room's faded magnificence. It was all exactly as she remembered. The ceiling was edged with an elaborate moulding and a single light bulb hung nakedly from an ornate rose in the centre. There were discoloured patches of damp on the golden yellow walls and the paintwork around the window was beginning to peel.

The girls started their warm up exercises at the barre.

"Turn those feet out. Heads to the left. Hold your chin up, Jemima. Nice straight backs. Oh Holly! It's the left foot first!"

Elinor Plank, the pianist, rushed into the studio breathlessly.

"So sorry Audrey, to be late, it was the baby, I was waiting for my husband, oh, I'll just start shall I?"

"Not to worry Mrs Plank," said Mrs Doyle, with a gracious wave of her hand. We're still warming up, but if you would be so kind as to play our entrance music, we can run through our dance. Thank you Mrs Plank! Oh and we have a visitor! Dear, dear Lucy; she can dance and play the piano too. One of my best pupils!"

Elinor smiled vaguely at Lucy, but her mind was still far away, hoping her husband was coping all right with their little baby daughter at home. She didn't like working on Saturday afternoon, but the show must go on.

Lucy smiled at Elinor sympathetically. Poor woman, she thought. She looks worn out. In Lucy's day, the pianist had been Mrs Doyle's mother, now sadly departed.

Elinor's fingers flew over the keys, deft and nimble, as the dancers cantered round the room, their eyes alight with excitement and energy.

What a wonderful pianist, thought Lucy. Lucky Audrey to find her after having to put up with her mother's playing for so many years. Mrs Doyle's mother had been completely resistant to taking any directions from her daughter and she was also rather deaf, whether by choice or by nature it was hard to tell, so the ballet classes had at times descended to a rather sordid clash of two mighty personalities. There had been no winners, but it had at least provided a great deal of amusement for the girls.

I'd quite like to play for ballet classes again myself, Lucy thought. She had done a lot of playing for classes when she had been a music student, to help support herself, but had given it all up when she had moved to Springfield for her first teaching job. I miss it, thought Lucy; it was such fun!

As the girls finished their dance, Mrs Doyle's husband, "The Major", popped his head round the door and stared into the room with bloodshot eyes. He was wearing an old tweed jacket and smelt strongly of whisky and tobacco.

"Just thought I'd see how you're getting on. My word, don't you young gels look pretty," he leered.

Time to go, thought Lucy. I'll sneak out now.

"Off you go upstairs, Horace," said Mrs Doyle crossly.

"You shouldn't be in here. Now girls, go to the back of the room and try your costumes on. Goodbye Lucy dear. See you tomorrow! Off you go Horace! The girls are changing!"

Horace "The Major" Doyle slunk away looking dejected but he perked up by the time he reached the upstairs sitting room as he remembered that he had recorded the Thunderbirds repeat last Tuesday. He could have some time to himself watching it on the television, before Audrey came upstairs.

"F.A.B." murmured The Major to himself. "Just F.A.B. An afternoon with Lady Penelope."

Lucy, having made her escape, walked briskly into the city centre, determined to make a good start to her Christmas shopping. She wandered in and out of exquisite little shops and boutiques, marvelling as always that Bath was such a beautiful and stylish city. Why do I live in Springfield, Lucy wondered for the umpteenth time. She went to her favourite toy shop which was crammed with all the things that parents want their children to have, beautifully designed, natural, educational and of course expensive toys. Rebecca and Teresa would prefer Barbies, thought Lucy. I know I would have. She didn't want to offend her sister by buying the twins something that Caroline disapproved of, but Caroline disapproved of so many things that Lucy felt she had a very narrow choice available to her.

Eventually Lucy found something suitable in a tiny gift shop in one of the cobbled passages right in the centre of the city, near the Abbey. It was a beautiful musical box snowstorm made of heavy glass with a tiny delicate ballerina inside, arms gracefully framing her face and one leg held out to the side at an almost improbable angle. The ballerina had downcast eyes and a demure smile. Lucy fell in love with her straight away and when she turned the key and discovered the music was from the Nutcracker, she knew it was the ideal present.

"Have you got two of them?" she asked eagerly. "Two the same? They're for twins you see. They have to have the same."

"Two?" echoed the assistant with a smile. "Two the same? Now let me see, yes, of course, here we are. Let me wrap them for you. Twins! How lovely!"

In Bakesville, Steve was also out shopping, but in his case it was food shopping for his parents. I'd better stock up for a couple of weeks, he thought. I've no idea when I'll be able to do a big shop again. I can get bits and pieces every day on my way back from work, of course. Now, let's see, have they got any of that wonderful ham that Mum likes so much?

Back in Bath, Caroline was battling her way through the Saturday afternoon crowds in her local supermarket. She usually tried to be more organised and get her shopping done during the week but she had been so busy over the last few days, what with the twins' dancing show coming up and Lucy's visit, that she'd forgotten to stock up with enough food.

With much manoeuvring and elbowing, Caroline finally made it to the fruit and vegetable display. She picked up a box of very dense, dark mushrooms, gazing intently at them, then reached out hesitantly for the ordinary closed cup mushrooms.

"Shiitake mushrooms are so now, all the chefs say so, but Rebecca and Teresa refused to eat them last time I cooked them in a risotto," Caroline mused aloud. The twins had complained that the Shiitake mushrooms had looked like slugs and were yucky and after that Caroline and Jeremy hadn't felt like eating them much either. No, decided Caroline. Not Shiitake mushrooms again. Maybe something completely different? She hovered over the ready-made pizzas, wondering if she dared to buy one. I should really make the pizza base, Caroline agonised.

Heavens, this is no good. I'll never get the shopping done at this rate. I've got to get a move on!

"I'm sure I read somewhere that it was OK for children to have the occasional ready meal," Caroline said to herself as she scooped up a packet of frozen chicken nuggets.

"After all, I can be flexible," she added with an anxious laugh. She remembered with a sudden flush of embarrassment how she had arrived to pick the twins up from a friend's party recently and had overheard one of the other mums say,

"Quick! It's Caroline! It's the food gestapo! Hide the crisps and hula hoops! They're full of additives and salt!"

Yes, thought Caroline angrily, I can be flexible and with that she positively charged back to the ready meals section and picked up two frozen pizzas and a rather small looking shepherd's pie that optimistically claimed it would feed a family of four. That'll show them, she thought. That will definitely show them.

Once her shopping was completed, Caroline dashed back to the Doyle Academy and picked up the girls. Driving home, she kept a look out for Lucy, in case they saw her walking back from her shopping and could give her a lift, but there was no sign of her,

"I think your Aunty Lucy's having a nice time shopping in the city," said Caroline to the twins happily.

"Oh bother," complained Rebecca. "Why isn't she on her way home yet?"

"Yes, I want to see Aunty Lucy," said Teresa with a pout.

"You two sound a bit tired to me," remarked Caroline. "I tell you what, I'll do you a quick supper then you can get ready for bed and sit up for a while in your dressing gowns and chat to Aunty Lucy. She's bound to be back soon."

"Yes!" shouted the twins in unison. "Yes, yes! We love Aunty Lucy!"

Lucy was at that moment making her way back through the city streets, trudging past the Abbey.

"Oh, I can hear music!" said Lucy in delight. "I'll just pop in to have a better listen."

She pushed open the massive door of the Abbey and made her way into the gloomy and dank interior. Her eyes took a few minutes to get accustomed to the darkness and then she could see a conductor in the distance, rehearsing with his choir of school children.

Not as good a conductor as Tristan, thought Lucy with sudden loyalty, but not bad either. Oh Tristan, she thought longingly, I wonder what you're doing now? Are you thinking about me? Are you planning to ask me out again? Lucy had completely forgotten about the more unsatisfactory aspects of her date with Tristan and was dwelling instead on the sheer romance and excitement of the evening. I know he loves me, thought Lucy. I'm not sure I love him yet, but I'm sure I will. He'll just have to prove himself. She suddenly thought of Steve's sad face as he had told her about his mother's illness. Why am I thinking about Steve, wondered Lucy. I hope all is well with his parents in Bakesville. Now, back to Tristan. Lucy closed her eyes and let the music drift over her.

"Remember me," sang the choir. "Remember me forever."

Lucy tried hard to remember what Tristan's face was like, but instead she kept remembering all the suggestive comments he had made during their evening out. Well, Tristan, thought Lucy, wrinkling her nose in distaste. I can see I'm going to have to change you. I wonder if you're having a good weekend?

Tristan was indeed having an excellent weekend. He was at that very moment in bed with Claire, having pursued her for such a long time. Nine out of ten, thought Tristan in delight. This is really wonderful. He had gone round to visit Claire that afternoon without any great expectations, after all, she had been somewhat offhand with him of late, but somehow one thing had led to another and they had both ended up in bed together.

"Oh Tristan," whispered Claire in his ear. "Oh Tristan, my darling."

Chapter Seven:
His wives and his concubines

Lucy, oblivious to this act of betrayal from her knight in shining armour, made her way back to Caroline's house in high spirits. Her image of Tristan was once again polished and perfect, all her doubts about his suitability swept away.

"I know I can change him, I know I can, I know I can," she chanted happily as she climbed up the steep hill to Caroline and Jeremy's large comfortable Victorian house.

"Aunty Lucy! Aunty Lucy! Oh, it's Aunty Lucy! At last!" shouted Rebecca.

"Yes, at last," echoed Teresa.

"We've been waiting so long, Aunty Lucy."

"Yes, so, so long!"

"We thought you'd never get back!"

"We thought you'd run off with someone," beamed Caroline. "Come in, Lucy, come in and look after these monsters for me. I can't cope any more!"

"They're not monsters: they're gorgeous!" said Lucy, trying to scoop Rebecca and Teresa up in her arms.

"I can't manage to pick you both up any more," she giggled, staggering under their weight. "What have you been eating?"

"Careful,' laughed Caroline. "I nearly put my back out last week trying to carry those two! It's strictly one at a time now they're getting so big."

"Daddy can carry us both," shouted Rebecca.

"Yes, Daddy is so strong, he's like Superman," remarked Teresa.

"Actually, Daddy is Superman," confided Rebecca. "He told me so last week."

"You don't want to believe everything a man tells you," laughed Caroline. "That goes for you too, Lucy –

you can't trust any of them!"

Except for my darling Tristan, thought Lucy with a secret smile. He'll never let me down.

Caroline was also thinking of Tristan. She'd been meaning to get round to talking to Lucy about him, ever since Sarah had told her what was going on. The man had a dreadful reputation and Caroline didn't want her little sister getting hurt. She had tried broaching the subject with Lucy on the phone the week before, but it hadn't gone very well. Jeremy had been no help at all; he had just said that in his opinion Lucy was old enough to take care of herself.

"You are so wrong," Caroline had said to her husband. "Lucy has always been a hopeless romantic, with silly dreams about wedding dresses and handsome young men."

"Well Tristan isn't young, so what's the problem?" Jeremy had remarked unhelpfully.

Caroline had sighed and given up at that point. She would have to try and sort it out herself.

Yes, thought Caroline as she watched Rebecca and Teresa dancing round Lucy in the hall; I really will have to have a chat with her about Tristan. Maybe I could try this evening if Rebecca and Teresa ever calm down enough to go to bed.

"Come into the kitchen, Lucy. I'll get you a drink," said Caroline. "Cup of tea? Or straight onto the wine? The children have already eaten and I'll get us something later."

"Oh, wine, I think," smiled Lucy. "I had a cup of tea in the city. I've done really well with Christmas shopping – I've got the girls a lovely present. Good heavens! What's that?"

Lucy pointed in amazement to a foil tray with a glutinous mass of brown and white stodge.

"That? Oh that!" said Caroline in confusion. "That's what I tried to give the girls for supper."

"Yes, I can see that," answered Lucy, "but what is it?"

"Supposedly shepherd's pie for four," laughed Caroline. "It's quite revolting and the girls point blank refused to eat it."

"Can't say I blame them," remarked Jeremy cheerfully, coming into the kitchen. "Can I have some of that wine? Why on earth did you buy that muck, if you don't mind me asking, my darling?"

"Well, to save time and for the convenience," answered Caroline. She explained to Jeremy and Lucy about the "food gestapo" comments she had overheard and had them both in fits of laughter.

"Of course, in the end it didn't save any time because I spent ages trying to convince the girls to eat it. They insisted that I had to taste it and once I'd tasted that bland wallpaper sweet stodgy taste, I said they didn't have to eat it and so then I cooked them a quick spaghetti carbonara."

"So you didn't save time and it certainly wasn't convenient," laughed Lucy.

"And I bet it cost twice as much as making it would have," commented Jeremy rather grouchily.

"Quiet you," warned Caroline. "You might have to eat it yourself if you don't behave."

"Oh no! Please!" gasped Jeremy in mock horror, clutching at his throat.

"What's wrong with Daddy?" asked Rebecca, flying into the room.

"Yes, what's wrong?" echoed Teresa. "Look Auntie Lucy, we've got our fairy wings on!"

And with that, the twins made a quick exit, before their mother could remember that they were supposed to be going to bed.

"If we had a dog, I suppose it might like to finish up the shepherd's pie?" suggested Caroline.

"No!" shouted Lucy and Jeremy in unison.

"Not even a dog would eat that!" cried Jeremy, by now wiping tears from his eyes, he was laughing so much.

"Straight into the bin," giggled Lucy.

"Yes!" said Caroline. "An end to my experiment of no cooking! Death to the ready meal!"

With that, she tipped the whole tray into the bin.

"Now, I'd better start cooking something for us," she said happily.

"I'll put the kids to bed," offered Jeremy. "Would you like to read their story, Lucy?"

"Try and stop me," grinned Lucy. "You know what a treat it is for me to see Rebecca and Teresa. I'll go up now and ask them what book they want."

"Books, not book, if I know them," said Caroline. "Don't let them take advantage of you, Lucy!"

And don't you let Tristan take advantage of you, either, Caroline thought more soberly. I must get round to that little chat this evening. Perhaps there will be time after supper.

"What story would you like, girls?" asked Lucy brightly as she finally located the twins in their hiding place behind the sofa. "Goodness, what pretty nighties!"

"Yes, mine's Little Mermaid and Rebecca's is Snow White," said Teresa proudly. "Look! They've got glitter on them!"

"They're all shiny! See how they sparkle," added Rebecca.

"Come on then," smiled Lucy. "You both look beautiful. Let's go upstairs. Shall we all sit in the same bed to have the story?"

"Yes, my bed!" shouted Rebecca.

"No, my bed," argued Teresa.

"One story in each bed?" suggested Lucy.

"My bed first," said Rebecca firmly.

"No, my bed…" began Teresa, but she dissolved into giggles when Lucy lay down on the floor and pretended to snore.

"I'm too tired," whimpered Lucy. "The more you argue, the more I shall snore."

"All right," said Rebecca graciously. "We'll go to

Teresa's bed first but we'll spend longer in my bed. We always spend longer in the second bed."

"Grr!" shouted Lucy, making her best monster face. "Grr! I'm chasing you to bed!"

When the three of them were happily tucked up in Teresa's bed, Lucy began the story.

"Once upon a time, there was a beautiful princess…"

Jeremy, Caroline and Lucy stayed up late that evening, enjoying their meal and putting the world to rights. Caroline never did get around to talking to her sister about Tristan. Shame to spoil the evening, she had thought after another glass of wine.

"You must come and stay with us more often," Jeremy said to Lucy. "The children are having the time of their lives." And you bring out the best in Caroline too, thought Jeremy with an affectionate look at his wife.

"Don't forget that you're invited for Christmas!" said Caroline. "I've told you Mum's staying, haven't I?"

"Thanks," replied Lucy simply. "I'd love to, that is, I'm sure I can spend part of the Christmas holiday with you. My plans aren't fixed yet." With that, she put her head down with a blush.

In Springfield, Claire pulled open her fridge door and peered inside. She gathered up all the little treats she had bought from that rather expensive delicatessen in town and arranged them on a tray with a bottle of champagne. Her flat mate was away for the weekend and Claire had known that Tristan would probably try to see her and so she had stocked up in anticipation. She had also bought herself a new red satin négligée a few days ago, in response to one of Tristan's looks during the choir rehearsal. Yes, she had thought, I think I can get him this weekend; get him and hang onto him if I play my cards right.

She carried the tray back to the bedroom, pushing the door open with her foot.

"Tristan!" she called softly. "Tristan! Wake up! I've got something for you."

"You certainly have," quipped Tristan. "Come here you gorgeous creature!"

"No! Not that!" laughed Claire. "I've brought you some food."

Tristan gazed in astonishment at the parma ham, greek olives, ciabatta, taramasalata and many more delicacies laid out in front of him.

"When did you, how did you, I mean, you didn't know I was definitely coming round did you?" he asked.

"I do eat when you're not here," retorted Claire sharply. "You're not one of those men who think women exist on no food, are you? Just the occasional scrap of cheese on toast and a few lettuce leaves? Oh, don't worry," continued Claire, with a rather strained laugh. "I'm only joking. Now, have some of that," she continued, handing him a glass of champagne. "That will put hairs on your chest."

Tristan stared down at his chest and felt very confused. Was Claire laughing at him? What was going on? He had thought that he had overwhelmed Claire with the force of his passion, on the spur of the moment. Could it be that she had planned the whole thing? Who cares, he thought with a sigh. It's wonderful!

"Here's to us," he said, clinking his glass against hers and reaching out for her. "You're utterly gorgeous," he murmured. "Come here you!"

Yes, thought Claire happily. All going according to plan so far. She was determined to become Mrs Proudfoot the third and to make sure there was no number four. All right, she knew Tristan wasn't perfect, but she wanted him, just as he was.

"And I think I know how to get you," she whispered.

"What was that?" asked Tristan.

"Nothing Tristan. Just a few sweet nothings I was whispering in your ear. I'm so glad you came round to see me today."

"So am I," leered Tristan. "Come here Claire, actually, wait a minute, I'm starving!"

Tristan sat up in bed and began gobbling the food Claire had brought him while she watched him with an indulgent smile.

"What is it they say about the way to a man's heart?" she laughed softly. "Go on Tristan, dig in; I'll be back in a minute."

Claire positively ran to the bathroom and took a small card of pills out of the bathroom cabinet. One by one, she popped them delicately into the basin until they were all gone, then ran some water to flush them away.

"Yes," she said happily. "All going according to plan!"

Thus it was that Lucy spent Saturday night dreaming of Tristan, while Claire lay in his arms.

On Sunday morning, Claire got up early and busied herself around the flat so that everything would look nice for Tristan when he woke up. She cooked him a vast breakfast of eggs, bacon, sausage, mushrooms, tomatoes and toast and sat watching him while he ate it.

"Wonderful coffee," enthused Tristan through a mouthful of food. "Wonderful breakfast!"

"That's all right," replied Claire happily. "After all, a man's got to keep his strength up, hasn't he?"

"Quite right, my darling," replied Tristan with one of his looks. "Quite right! No complaints so far, I hope?"

"None," sighed Claire contentedly. "But don't you get too conceited, Tristan! Now, what are we going to do today?"

"Well," ventured Tristan cautiously, "I thought I might nip home and do some work. Concert's coming up, you know. Things to plan, things to organise!"

"Good, then I'll come with you," replied Claire.

Now that she had hooked her man, she wasn't going

to be foolish enough to let him out of her sight.

"Oh, I don't think..." Tristan began, but Claire had already rushed off to have her shower, singing snatches of Belshazzar as she went.

"In that night was Belshazzar the King slain, slain!"

Tristan was puzzled. Why is she singing that, he wondered; it isn't even a soprano line. He began to feel vaguely uneasy and hoped Claire wouldn't stay too long at his place as he planned to ring Lucy later on to see if she was back from her weekend. He finished his breakfast thoughtfully, wondering what he was getting himself into.

"Come on Tristan," said Claire happily, appearing in the kitchen fully dressed with a beaming smile on her face. She began rummaging in the cupboard under the sink and chucking things into a carrier bag.

"What on earth are you doing?" asked Tristan in astonishment.

"Just taking a few things round to your place," answered Claire brightly. "I thought I could do a bit of tidying up for you while you do your work. I know how you bachelors live," she continued archly. "I bet your place needs a woman's touch. Now come on, get showered and dressed and then you can help me carry this stuff to the car. I can't manage these bags and the hoover as well. Hurry up! Hurry up Tristan, or the whole morning will be wasted!"

Tristan made his way to the shower, completely bewildered.

"And I thought you could take me out to lunch today," Claire called after him. "You know, to that lovely place out in the country you took me to once before. Do you remember? Or we could make it dinner. Whatever you want."

Do I remember, Tristan thought ruefully. Why, she slapped my face last time I took her there. What has got into the woman?

"Great idea," said Tristan. "But perhaps we could

come back here for a meal?"

"No," said Claire firmly. "You're taking me out."

Tristan stumbled into the bedroom to look for his clothes. They weren't where he'd left them, scattered over the floor. Where could they be? Then he noticed them neatly arranged on a chair.

"Everything all right?" asked Claire brightly, popping her head round the door. "Aren't you going to have a shower? You'd better get a move on because I'm nearly ready to go."

Tristan drove Claire back to his house in a daze. As he swung into the large drive, Claire cried out with pleasure.

"Oh Tristan! What a lovely house! But it needs some attention, you know. Isn't it time you got the window frames painted? And your front garden is rather overgrown."

"Well, it was my parents' house," said Tristan. "They kept it beautifully but I'm so busy, I just don't get the time. It is a bit neglected, like me I suppose. Are you going to give me lots of attention Claire? I need a lot of pampering, you know. I need wrapping in cotton wool."

"All in good time," answered Claire, hopping out of the car with her bags of cleaning stuff. "All in good time. Now, don't let me stop you doing your music; I'll be quite happy whizzing round the house with the hoover." And I can have a good look round too, thought Claire. Get to know you a bit better, Tristan!

To Tristan's amazement, he soon found himself sitting at his piano studying scores, with freshly brewed coffee beside him and a plate of his favourite custard creams.

"This is like the coffee at your place," he said to Claire in astonishment.

"It is the coffee from my place," laughed Claire. "I don't leave things to chance! Enjoy the custard creams! Did you know that I once heard someone at choir calling me Miss Custard Cream?"

"No," said Tristan vaguely.

"Well I did," continued Claire. "It was that new girl, Lucy. Do you know her?"

"I think so," replied Tristan, putting his head down and taking a large bite of custard cream.

"She thought I didn't hear her, but she called me Miss Custard Cream after she saw me feeding you custard creams at choir recently. Still, who cares! I've been called worse," Claire continued cheerfully. "At least I'm not a little milksop like her."

"Lucy's a lovely girl," protested Tristan.

Whoops, thought Claire; I'd better tread carefully here.

"Of course she is," she said hastily. "It's just that she's not really my type, or yours either I would have thought. Anyway I'll leave you to it."

Claire shut the sitting room door with a bang and Tristan was soon lost in his music. His hands grasped strongly at the chords as he played Belshazzar's Feast on his piano, singing various parts as he went along. He hadn't done any serious work on his music for ages and he had forgotten how good it made him feel.

Claire acquainted herself with every room in the house and then began her cleaning in earnest. It was quite a challenge and as she dusted and polished, scoured and scrubbed, she hoped it would all be worth it. The floors were so dusty that she had to empty the hoover bag half way through her efforts. Really, she thought, you'd think a genius would be able to keep his house in a better state than this. The kitchen was the worst room in the house, closely followed by the bathroom. I won't be able to finish today, she thought crossly; it would take at least a day to tackle just those two rooms. Down in the cellar, she found Tristan's spare house keys and on an impulse, slipped them into her pocket. I've got some time next week, she thought. I'm owed some holiday at work and I can afford to take a day off to come and sort this place out. I'll just have to find out when Tristan will be out. She knew that in addition to his choir work, he had various other commitments during the week, some adult education classes and some piano teaching in one of the private boys' schools in the south of Springfield. She also remembered that he was planning to spend Wednesday up in London, some freelance work in the BBC studios at Maida Vale she thought, so that could be a useful day for her to come round, do some spring cleaning and then go straight on to choir practice.

Claire worked as a secretary in a solicitor's office in the centre of Springfield. She enjoyed her job and had been there for ten years, but didn't want to do it for ever. I've got other plans, she hummed to herself happily as she attacked the burned on food debris on Tristan's cooker hob.

"I've got other plans, other plans…"

"Make a joyful noise," Tristan bellowed in the sitting room, "unto the God of Jacob."

He was practising his conducting in front of a full length mirror to the right of the piano.

"Magnificent!" he shouted, gazing at himself in the mirror, eyes alight and dark locks flowing around his head like a halo.

"Absolutely magnificent performance!"

He leapt back to the piano and began pounding out the orchestral reduction on the keyboard with wild passion if not great accuracy.

"Magnificent," echoed Claire, scrubbing happily at the oven. "He really is a genius."

Lucy too was thinking about Tristan as she sat in Caroline's kitchen. How talented he is, she thought. I can't wait for the rehearsal next Wednesday! Perhaps he will ring me before then, she wondered. I do hope so!

Her thoughts were interrupted by the excited chatter of the twins. Their dancing show was at three o'clock that very afternoon and Caroline was finding it difficult to get the girls to eat an early lunch.

"You need to keep your strength up. Just have a little bit of food, please," she begged the twins.

"Oh, leave them alone," snapped Jeremy, uncharacteristically grumpy this morning.

"Too much wine last night my darling?" asked Caroline sympathetically.

"Yes, sorry Caroline. I am feeling a bit delicate; sorry to snap," apologised Jeremy. "Come on girls: you can manage a sandwich, can't you?"

"Oh all right," said Teresa graciously. "Since Daddy asked me to."

"Yes," echoed Rebecca. "I will too, because I want to build up my strength and dance my very, very best, especially because Aunty Lucy is going to be there watching us."

"I can't wait!" smiled Lucy. "Your end of term show!"

"Have you got our costumes ready, Mummy?" asked Teresa.

"I'll just go and check your bags," promised Caroline hastily. "You're changing there, aren't you? Good. Yes Rebecca, I do know your hair has to be done at home. I'm hoping Lucy will do that again for you."

"Aunty Lucy! Aunty Lucy!" the twins cried. "We love having you here!"

After lunch, Lucy put the twins' hair up in two identical buns, with little crowns made of pipe cleaners pinned onto the top. She had to use quite a few hair grips to pin back the pieces of hair at the sides as neither twin had really long hair, but Mrs Doyle had said that all girls must have their hair scraped back from their faces, so it had to be done.

"I wish I had hair down to my waist like Hermione," sighed Rebecca.

"Yes, she can nearly sit on her hair," said Teresa.

"Well I can sit on your hair if I sit on your head," shrieked Rebecca. "Come on, let's try!"

"Girls," implored Lucy, "just sit still a bit longer.

Come on, just a few more hair grips. You want to look gorgeous, don't you?"

"May we have hairspray again?" asked Rebecca.

"Yes! Yes, hairspray Aunty Lucy!" shouted Teresa.

"Well, maybe a little," laughed Lucy. "It does help to keep everything in place. Now, shut your eyes both of you. I'm going to put my hand over your eyes and spray. There, all done!"

Lucy looked at the girls admiringly.

"I think I've done a pretty good job here."

"Yuk!" said Teresa. "What a funny smell that hairspray is. I wouldn't want to use that every day."

"Only ladies do that," advised Rebecca, "so don't worry because you're not a lady yet."

"Not all ladies use hairspray," laughed Lucy. "It's for special occasions really."

"Like when you get married?" asked Rebecca.

"Yes, I suppose so," answered Lucy with a blush.

"Can we be bridesmaids when you get married?" asked Teresa.

"I wouldn't choose anyone else," smiled Lucy, "but I don't have any plans to get married at the moment."

"Just as well," was Caroline's comment as she dashed into the room. "You don't want to get married too early, do you? Now come on girls; your carriage awaits. Oh! You do look so sweet! Let me cuddle you."

"Better not," said Rebecca gravely.

"Yes," said Teresa. "We don't want our hair messed up. It took Aunty Lucy ages to do and you might hurt her feelings if it's messed up."

The two girls walked solemnly from the room while Caroline and Lucy followed, giggling uncontrollably.

"What are you two laughing at?" asked Jeremy as he ran down the stairs.

"We'll tell you in the car," said Caroline, wiping tears of laughter from her eyes. "Those daughters of yours, honestly, they're priceless! Come on. We'd better get going now."

The show was to take place in a church hall near the Doyle Academy where Lucy herself had danced on many occasions in the past. Caroline and Jeremy took their places in the audience while Lucy went backstage with the twins to help them into their costumes.

"Lucy, darling," boomed Audrey Doyle. "How lovely of you to help. We can always do with an extra pair of hands!"

The pianist, Elinor Plank, was there too, helping girls into tutus and pink satin shoes.

"It's going to be a wonderful show, girls," trilled Mrs Doyle. "You're all in tiptop form! Just do your best. I'm so proud of you all!"

Lucy took her place next to Caroline and Jeremy in the audience and Elinor sat down at the piano just to the left of the red velvet curtains. As the introduction rang out, the curtains opened to reveal a dazzling display of girls in sparkly green and yellow costumes.

"Ah!" breathed the audience.

Elinor's husband, Tom, was in the audience with their baby, Alice. Tom gazed at his wife with great pride as she kept the show together, fingers flying over the keys. Baby Alice bounced on Tom's knee and Tom encircled her in his arms and gently nuzzled the top of her head. Alice put one arm around his neck and stretched the other hand out to the stage and pointed at the spectacle in front of her. She gazed with wide eyes and open mouth at the girls in their gorgeous tutus; she had never seen anything as beautiful as this before. It was like a great sea of frothy green and yellow.

Hermione fell over with a bump at one point but she was soon up and on her feet again. Rebecca and Teresa managed beautifully, both frowning a little with concentration as they galloped round in a circle. Lucy could see a tear glistening on Caroline's cheek and felt rather overwhelmed herself.

"The Major" was sitting in the front row, snoozing, his moustache vibrating softly as he breathed in and out.

"He'd better not snore," warned Mrs Doyle sharply, peering out from behind the curtain. "I won't have him snoring! Maybe I should have left him watching his old videos at home."

All too soon, the show was over and the girls were streaming into the audience to be congratulated by their proud parents.

"Marvellous you two, simply marvellous," boomed Jeremy, scooping Rebecca and Teresa up into his arms.

The twins smiled happily as Caroline and Lucy added their praise.

"I'm bursting with pride, just absolutely bursting," enthused Lucy.

"Oh Aunty Lucy," said Rebecca, "please don't go home; stay longer!"

"I'd love to sweetie, but I'm working tomorrow," smiled Lucy. "I've got to catch that train; I'm so sorry."

"Talking of trains," said Caroline anxiously, "we'd better get you to the station. Your bag's in the car, isn't it? Good. We'll drop you off on our way home. Now you're sure you'll be OK? I do hope you won't get home too late."

"I'll be fine," smiled Lucy. "And thanks for a really wonderful weekend."

The journey to the station passed in minutes and all too soon Lucy was saying her final goodbyes.

"Be sure to ring as soon as you get in!" called Caroline out of the car window as Lucy disappeared into the station clutching her weekend bag. "We want to know you've arrived home safely!"

Bother, thought Caroline, I never did find the time to have a chat with Lucy about Tristan. Oh well, I'll try on the phone sometime.

"Home darling!" Caroline said to Jeremy. "Aren't you proud of your two darling daughters?"

"Very," replied Jeremy. "Early bed for the pair of them, I think," he continued, ignoring the squeals of protest from the back of the car, "and then maybe I might even get to spend a little time with my wife on our own!"

"Lovely darling," sighed Caroline and she put her hand on his leg as they drove up the hill home. Rebecca and Teresa looked at each other and giggled, then pretended to be sick.

Lucy didn't have long to wait for the London train. As she saw it approaching the platform a wild thought came into her head. I could miss it, she thought. I could miss it and not go back to Springfield. I wouldn't have to teach all those classes next week. Lucy had put her teaching firmly to the back of her mind all weekend, determined to have a complete break from it, but unfortunately now that all too familiar Sunday evening nausea was creeping over her. I can't face it, she thought, panic stricken. I just can't face it and I haven't prepared my lessons properly for tomorrow anyway. I don't even know how to prepare for some of my classes and I don't want to do it any more. I'll do anything else. I could be a waitress or work in a library or give hundreds of piano lessons. I'll do anything; I just can't face going back.

Lucy boarded the train with the other passengers, as she had known all along that she would. You'll feel better, she told herself, as soon as you get into the swing of things next week. You know Sunday evenings are always bad. Anyway, what have I got to complain about, she thought, cheering up a bit as the train picked up speed. I'm perfectly healthy, I've got a nice place to live, with a flatmate I like, I'm in a great choir and it's the concert soon. And before that, it's the party at Grangewood too, she remembered with delight. I'd better remind Tristan about coming to the party, after all it's next Saturday. Not long now; I wonder what I should wear? Lucy spent the next half an hour mentally scanning the contents of both her own and Julia's wardrobes, trying to think what she would look the most alluring in. She then fell asleep.

Diagonally opposite Lucy, on the other side of the carriage, sat a well dressed man in his late fifties who had noticed Lucy from the moment she boarded the train. He had joined the train in Bristol and was on his way back to London after visiting friends for the weekend.

"A real pre-Raphaelite beauty," the man breathed to himself. "Just look at that hair!" As Lucy slept, he took a pencil and sketchbook out of his bag and rapidly began to capture her likeness. He copied faithfully the curve of her lips, her slightly aquiline nose, the shape of her eyelashes as she slept and the mass of red hair that swept back from her face and down over her shoulders. His interest in Lucy's beauty was purely professional, for Robert Nibbet, or Bob to his friends, was an artist working in London, well known for many years both within his circle and to a wider audience. He carried his sketchbook with him constantly, always on the lookout for interesting and beautiful sights and in Lucy he thought he had found perfection.

"Excuse me," Bob said to Lucy as the train pulled into Paddington. "Excuse me, I hope you don't think…"

Lucy woke with a start and rubbed her eyes.

"Oh!" she cried. "Oh, I've been asleep. Thank you for waking me." She gave Robert a beaming smile.

"I hope you don't mind," continued Robert, "but I thought I'd better let you know we had reached the end of the line. If you stay on the train, you'll probably be back in the West Country again in no time."

"I wouldn't mind, actually," said Lucy. "But thanks anyway. Oh, what's this? Surely it's not, oh, how embarrassing, oh, I don't know what to say!"

Lucy blushed as she stared at the sketch in front of her.

"Is that really me?" she asked, her face scarlet by now.

"You have a most interesting face," said Bob gravely.

"Most interesting, very fine eyes; pity they were shut when I sketched you! No, please keep the sketch if it is of any interest to you. I will carry your likeness in my head now. So nice to have met you my dear; goodbye, goodbye."

With a quaint shake of her hand, Bob Nibbet was on his way, leaving an astonished Lucy holding her portrait.

My goodness, she thought, what an end to a weekend. She tucked the portrait into her bag, taking care not to squash it and made her way to the underground to get to Victoria and then to Springfield. Once home, she propped the sketch behind a vase on the mantle piece in the sitting room.

"Blimey!" said Julia when she saw it. "Flatters you, doesn't it! Only joking; it's a very good likeness. Where did you get it from?"

Lucy explained about her encounter on the train.

"Sounds like a new chat up line to me!" Julia laughed.

"Oh no," said Lucy, "it wasn't like that, I mean, he was old."

"Like Tristan," retorted Julia.

"No," replied Lucy rather primly. "Much older."

"Only joking," said Julia, still laughing. "Look, I'm just making some pasta; do you fancy some?"

"Great," said Lucy. "It's been a long time since lunch. Thanks! I'll just give Caroline a quick ring to say I've arrived safely, then we can eat and have a good gossip. I want to hear about your weekend, Julia and how many hearts you've broken!"

As Lucy and Julia sat down to their pasta, Tristan and Claire were also sharing a meal, at Castle Temple, where Tristan had taken Lucy only two days before.

Tristan didn't notice the raised eyebrows and the meaningful glances of the staff at Castle Temple as he sat at his table with Claire. He was too busy feeling happy. The weekend had been perfect so far, with the unexpected pleasures of Saturday, then a whole day studying his music and now a fabulous meal in his favourite restaurant. Claire had seemed quite happy cleaning his house for him and she had done marvels in a short space of time. Tristan felt that he owed her this meal. It was the least that he could do.

He had chosen his favourite dish, steak and had been surprised that Claire had chosen exactly the same. They both sat opposite each other, not talking but tearing at their meat with obvious enjoyment.

"I've never known a woman who enjoyed her food as much as you do, Claire," commented Tristan in astonishment.

"Well, why shouldn't I?" retorted Claire. "I don't want to be stick thin or get anorexia. What's wrong with a real woman's figure?"

"Nothing at all my darling," drooled Tristan as he ogled her opulent curves. "Nothing at all."

"Well then," said Claire in satisfaction. "Ooo! Look at those deserts, Tristan!" she continued, licking her lips. "Let's have something wicked!"

After they had eaten their fill, Tristan suggested a walk in the gardens, just as he had with Lucy.

"That's an improvement Tristan!" laughed Claire. "Last time you tried to get me to stay the night in one of the hotel bedrooms! You're being very chivalrous tonight."

"Mm, yes," mumbled Tristan. "I seem to remember something like that…"

"Seem to remember that I slapped you hard across the face, you idiot," shrieked Claire, bellowing with laughter by now.

"Quick, let's go outside," said Tristan urgently. He was suddenly aware of other diners staring at Claire. "I think you've had rather a lot of champagne. I'll just pay the bill while you wait outside."

Claire and Tristan embraced passionately in the gardens, not noticing how cold it was. Tristan wisely did not try to take Claire through the rose bushes as he had done with Lucy, but found a path this time.

"This way," he whispered softly to Claire. "This way; let me hold you again."

As Claire looked over Tristan's shoulder she could see the water nymph statue lying on the ground.

"Oh look," she said "Look through that arch, Tristan; there's a statue. It must have blown over in the wind. Let's put it back on its little platform."

Tristan and Claire went through the arch hand in hand and then between them pulled the statue back into position. The water nymph did not seem grateful, but regarded Tristan with a reproachful eye. Tristan stuck his tongue out at her.

"Let's go home," he suggested to Claire. "Come on; you're shivering. Let's go home to bed."

"Last one to the car's an idiot," shrieked Claire, running back through the arch and along the path. "Come on Tristan. You're so slow!"

Tristan puffed after her. Must cut down on the cigarettes, he thought. Now, where's that woman disappeared to?

The waiter looked out of the dining room window, alerted by the sound of Claire's cries, just in time to see her running from the garden with Tristan in hot pursuit.

The waiter gave a knowing smirk and winked at one of his colleagues.

"That Mr Proudfoot," he jeered with a coarse laugh, "he really is a one. Mind you, I think he's met his match at last, definitely met his match!"

Chapter Eight: Thou art weighed in the balance and found wanting

"Party at Grangewood Golf Club," Steve read on the notice board at school. He rubbed his eyes, feeling tired after commuting from his parents' cottage to school. And this is only Wednesday, he thought ruefully; I've only been doing the journey for two days so far!

He had almost forgotten about the party at the golf club but now he remembered with a surge of emotion that Lucy had said she would be there.

"I'll see her at choir tonight too," he said to himself. "Things are looking up!"

Steve's father had insisted that Steve must not give up on his own life, in particular the Springfield Choral Society, so Steve was going to go to the choir rehearsal this evening and then stay the night at his own flat in Springfield, instead of driving back to his parents.

"I'll have a chance to pick up a few things," said Steve, still staring at the notice board in the staff room of his school. "I think I should probably take some more clean shirts this time... Good old Dad; he knows how important choir is to me, or should I say how important it is for me to see Lucy! She's the one bright spot in my life right now!"

"Hey, Steve mate, you all right?" shouted a colleague lounging in an armchair. "The bell's gone, you know and I've been watching you; you've been staring at that notice board as if you're in a trance!"

"It's OK thanks," said Steve, turning round. "I'm free first lesson, anyway."

"You're not free, you know," said the colleague, bounding up to the notice board and jabbing his finger at a small scruffy timetable. "Look, you're covering first lesson in the Art Department. That will be that new teacher away again, she's always ill, that Miss, oh, what's her name? Nice legs."

"Miss Henshaw," said Steve. "Bother, why didn't I look at the cover for the day? I'll just get my marking and rush down there."

"No you won't, mate," said his colleague with unexpected thoughtfulness. "You sit there and have a strong coffee. You look done in. I know you. You're always overdoing things and all this commuting is too much for you. I'll cover the lesson."

"Thanks," said Steve gratefully. "Thanks Mark. I owe you a drink."

"Too right mate," shouted Mark as he ran for the door. "And you can buy it for me at the party at Grangewood on Saturday."

Ah yes, thought Steve, the party at Grangewood. I think I'll give Lucy a ring to remind her about it.

Then Steve remembered that he had already rung Lucy the previous Monday and she had said that she had tickets for the party. Steve supposed that Lucy was going with her flat mate, Julia. Lucy had mentioned Julia a few times and had said how well the two of them got on and Steve knew that Julia also taught at Lucy's school so it would seem the logical thing for Lucy and Julia to go to the party together, Steve reasoned.

Perhaps I could ring Lucy about something else, Steve wondered, but she's bound to be teaching now, either that or rehearsing, after all, a music teacher's busiest time is the end of the Christmas term, or so my colleagues in the Music Department keep telling me.

Steve secretly hoped that Lucy would ask him to her school Christmas Concert. He must remember to ask her about it when he saw her at choir tonight. With a large sigh, Steve sat down and began looking at a pile of work on the Tudors.

"Henry the Eighth," Steve read, "cut people's heads off as much as he could because then he could do whatever he wanted."

Not a bad idea, thought Steve. Perhaps I could cut Tristan's head off for starters.

"Here you are, Steve; you look as if you need this," said a beaming middle aged lady, plonking a steaming mug of instant coffee in front of Steve, with three shortbread fingers on a plate.

"I've sweetened the coffee, just two spoonfuls; even if you don't take sugar, you need it, Steve. You look shattered," continued the lady who was Steve's Head of Department, Hermione Trubshaw, a very splendid teacher who had been at the school since the year dot and who took a keen interest in the well being of all her staff. Steve in particular brought out all her mothering qualities, especially now that he had dark bags under his eyes, ruffled hair and an obviously un-ironed shirt.

"Tell me what's going on," commanded Hermione, as she placed a large jewelled hand on his shoulder. "I insist on knowing. It's woman trouble, isn't it?"

"Well, sort of," laughed Steve uneasily, not quite sure he wanted to confide in Hermione, but he gave in as he knew he wouldn't get a moment's peace until he did.

"It's my mother," said Steve simply.

"Your mother?" Hermione echoed. "But I thought she was over all that. Why didn't you say, my dear boy? What's going on? Tell me all."

Steve soon found himself confiding in Hermione about his mother's setbacks and his father's anxieties and exhaustion.

"And so I've moved in with them for a while," explained Steve. "I'll be all right once I've got used to the travelling and it's nearly the end of term anyway, only another couple of weeks or so."

"You are a very special son," breathed Hermione in admiration. "Why, if only my Anton was more like you, but no, I mustn't criticise. He does his best, poor lamb and it's not been easy for him since my dear husband was taken from us, but anyway, enough of that; it's you, you Steve that we must concentrate on. You just let me know if you need anything, perhaps the odd lesson covered last thing in the day so that you can nip off early to beat the traffic? Good, good, now I'll leave you in peace, dear boy, to finish your work."

In pieces, more likely, thought Steve, but he felt cheered by Hermione's support, however comically she had given it.

Steve managed to keep going for the rest of the day, buoyed up by the thought of choir and Lucy; in fact his lessons went well, unlike Lucy's. She was having a very tough time with her Year 8 class in the afternoon. Why did I plan to do singing, she wondered. They're far too excitable this afternoon; surely no one could control them?

"Sit down," she shouted over the din. "Now, you know that we've got to go over these carols for the carol service at the end of term, now, sit down I said. Tom! Joe! Sit down I said!"

Just then, Mary Goodshoe swept into the room and an immediate silence fell over the classroom as the children froze.

"Oh, excuse me, Miss Lavender," began Mary. "I wondered if we should rehearse the carols together, that is, if you like. It would be so useful for me, dear and I could take the rehearsal and you could play for us; I do so like it when you accompany."

"Great!" answered Lucy. "We'll join classes straightaway if you like."

Mrs Goodshoe sighed in relief. She had been trying to do some listening work with her Year 7 class next door to Lucy's class and as the music department walls seemed to be made out of thin cardboard, she was not having much success battling against the row from Lucy's class. The school carol service was coming up soon and it wouldn't do any harm to have an extra rehearsal for the two classes.

"Now," boomed Mrs Goodshoe, "single file Year 8, single file into my classroom. Yes, Tom, I know it's a squash, but you'll still have room to breathe, I promise you."

"More's the pity," spluttered Lucy under her breath and then blushed scarlet, feeling rather ashamed of herself.

Mary Goodshoe's teaching room was larger than Lucy's, with a carpeted rehearsal area behind the desks, just big enough to accommodate the two classes if they sat sensibly on the floor.

"Rosie! Rosie!" called Mrs Goodshoe sharply. "Don't try to trip people up, there's a dear. Now we'll all sing through a few carols sitting down, to make sure of the notes, then we can have a full performance standing up at the end of the lesson. Sassy! Would you mind opening the window? Thank you. Yes, Jake, I know it's the beginning of December, but you'll soon warm up once we start singing."

Soon the two classes were singing with gusto. Mrs Goodshoe stood in front of them, mouthing the words and jabbing one finger skywards.

"A little higher, class! Watch that breathing!"

"Mary was that mother mild," bellowed the children.

Lucy's fingers scampered up and down the keyboard as she improvised a descant over the melody.

Mrs Goodshoe was impressed with Lucy's playing, as were the children. Pity she's got no control over the class, mused Mary Goodshoe. She couldn't quite decide whether Lucy was an inexperienced teacher with potential, or a talented musician who shouldn't be in class teaching.

"Now children," said Mrs Goodshoe, "you know that we've had a school carol competition, well, I'm going to let you be the first two classes to learn to sing the winning carol. It's a really lovely piece of music by one of the GCSE Music group and Miss Lavender has very cleverly put a piano part to it. Thank you Miss Lavender! Tom, look this way please and now could you pass those sheets along, yes, you Emma, quickly now and let's all read the words through together."

"It was so cold and snowy," the class read solemnly,

"And the robins looked so bonny."

"Yes, yes," said Mrs Goodshoe hurriedly, "I know it doesn't quite rhyme, but that's not the point, is it Emma? It's known as poetic licence in the trade and this is how the first line goes. Thank you Miss Lavender."

Mary Goodshoe threw her head back and sang in a rich and wobbly soprano voice,

"It was so cold and snowy

And the robins looked so bonny."

There were a few giggles from some boys in the back row but most of the class were open mouthed in astonishment.

"'ere. Mrs Goodshoe! You sound like one of them opera singers, a bit like that kiwi lady I seen on the telly. You know the one?"

"Yes, yes, thank you Jason," said Mrs Goodshoe graciously. "Now let's see if you can all sing that."

The children sang the simple melody back, a few of them with extra vibrato and a good measure of head tossing which Mrs Goodshoe thought it wisest not to comment on.

Why, my Year 8s are having a great time, thought Lucy in amazement. I was convinced they hated music, but it must be me they hate or at least my lessons. Lucy continued with her sad and self pitying thoughts as her fingers picked out the accompaniment on automatic pilot.

"Cor, that was the best music lesson ever," she heard one of her class say as they streamed out of the lesson. "I wish we always had our lessons together with the other class and Mrs Goodshoe."

"It's the novelty value," whispered Mary to a crestfallen Lucy as the last of the children hurried off to their next lesson. "But actually, if you don't mind, perhaps we could combine a few more classes until the carol service, as they could do with some extra rehearsal time. What do you think?"

"Great!" enthused Lucy. "I'd much rather accompany them than teach them. I mean, that is, if it would help, then of course I don't mind sacrificing the lessons and I'm sure we can catch up next term."

"I wonder you didn't think of earning your living by accompanying and piano teaching," was Mary's next comment. "You are so talented, you know."

"I suppose I thought I should have a steady job," replied Lucy. "Also, to be honest, everyone seemed to assume that I'd go into teaching because I love children and I love music."

"Yes dear," continued Mary, "but there are different sorts of teaching, aren't there? Class teaching isn't the only way to use your talents."

"Don't you think I'm any good at class teaching?" asked Lucy. "I'd prefer you to be honest. Just tell me."

"Well," started Mary cautiously and then continued in quick relief, "Oh Jason, you've come back have you? Forgotten your bag? Yes dear, here it is. You run along now, quick as you can, yes dear, off you go. I must dash too, Lucy; we'll finish our little conversation some other time, dear. Off I go!"

Lucy stared at Mary's retreating form in amazement. At last, she thought, at last we were really getting somewhere. Mary was giving me some useful advice, no holds barred and then suddenly she's off.

"Coward!" muttered Mary to herself as she beetled up the corridor. "Coward, that's all I am, a big coward; it's just that I don't want to upset that poor girl." Mary slowed down a little, out of breath now and continued her agonising.

"But I should have laid it on the line, really I should, it's not fair to the children, or to Lucy, to keep on covering up for her. I've got to see the Head, Mr Inchwood, this week and he's bound to ask how Lucy is doing. Oh, I'm going to have to be cruel to be kind and I'm going to do it now!"

Mary bumbled back to her room with a strong resolve, hoping that Lucy would still be there, but Lucy had vanished, probably to the staff room Mary thought.

"Bother, bother and bother," Mary complained. "And bother again. Still, I can use my time sensibly now I'm here, after all, I've plenty to get on with."

Humming to herself, Mary started to tackle one of her favourite tasks, covering new song books in sticky backed plastic.

"Tra la," sang Mary as her scissors snipped neatly and then,

"The robins looked so bonny," she continued, lining up the plastic carefully on the books.

Lucy, meanwhile, was in tears in the staff room, being comforted by Julia.

"She's got no right to talk to you like that," was Julia's indignant comment.

"Yes she has," snuffled Lucy. "She's my Head of Department and I wish she'd been more honest earlier, I really do you know. I feel as if I've been battling on, floundering about out of my depth and up to my neck in trouble."

"That sounds jolly uncomfortable," laughed Julia. "Oh come on, Lucy, that's better. Let's talk about it tonight, shall we? I've got to dash: I'm teaching in a few minutes, but we'll talk tonight, OK?"

"I'm going to choir tonight," smiled Lucy. "The one bright spot of my week."

Before choir, Lucy went next door to No 47, Angela's house. She had promised to help Angela learn some of the notes of Belshazzar and in return Angela had asked Lucy to have a quick bite to eat with her and Amy before choir.

Amy was delighted to see Lucy.

"Shall I play my piano piece?" she asked. "I'm very,

very clever at the piano."

"I know you are, darling," laughed Lucy, "but I've come to help your Mummy today."

"Yes, Amy, my turn," said Angela cheerfully. "Your lesson is on Monday. Now, are you going to sit on Mummy's knee while we do some work? Yes? Come on then, sweetie."

Amy climbed onto Angela's knee and they both gazed in amazement as Lucy started playing the opening of Belshazzar.

"The tenors and basses sing this," explained Lucy as the strange chords rang out. "Your first entry is after this gentler section."

"It's scary, Mummy," said Amy, hiding her head in Angela's blouse. "It's ghostie music."

"Here's your note Angela," said Lucy, "after two, with me."

"By the wa-----ters of Babylon," they both sang.

"Now, watch that top F," warned Lucy. "Support from your diaphragm, that's it; let's try it again, shall we? Oh good, yes, it's better each time, it's just a question of confidence."

"You amaze me," said Angela when they were sitting down to a generous helping of shepherd's pie later. "You truly amaze me; you're so talented!"

"I don't feel as if I can use all my talents at school, you know," said Lucy sadly.

"Pearls before swine, is it?" asked Angela. "A common problem in teaching, I believe."

"Actually," admitted Lucy candidly, "I'm don't seem to be very good at discipline yet. I suppose it will come."

"Don't like this," moaned Amy, stirring her shepherd's pie contemptuously. "What is it?"

"It's shepherd's pie, your favourite," commented Angela dryly.

"Ooo, shepherd's pie! I love it!" shrieked Amy. "Lucy, I love shepherd's pie, I do. Can I have yours?"

"Just eat your own first," laughed Angela, turning to talk to Lucy again. Amy stole a couple of carrots from her mother's plate when she thought she wasn't looking and Angela and Lucy winked at each other. Before they had finished eating, the phone rang.

"Hello Angela, darling," said Jeffrey. "I'm afraid a few things have come up at the office and I've got to stay on and sort them out. Yes, I do know it's your choir evening and you want me home as soon as possible, but it can't be helped. I'll be as quick as I can."

"You'd better go on to choir without me," said Angela sadly. "Perhaps you could tell Deborah that I'll be there as soon as I can. Oh, what a nuisance! Still, Jeffrey can't help it; these things happen. Anyway," she continued, "once Amy's in bed, I can have an extra note bash and try to put into practice all your good advice about that opening chorus, can't I?"

"I'll see you later then Angela," said Lucy, "and thank you so much for the meal and thank you Amy for the cabaret!"

"Oh, I should be thanking you, Lucy," replied Angela. "I feel as if I know Belshazzar so much better now. Thanks Lucy! Don't be late for choir, will you. See you there!"

Lucy hurried back to No. 49. Choir! I'll soon be at choir with Tristan! Should I change my clothes, Lucy wondered, or do I look OK? Perhaps some more lipstick and definitely that gorgeous perfume I wore when he took me out last Friday.

Lucy hummed to herself as she scrabbled through a little basket full of lipsticks that she kept on her dressing table. Perfect Pink, she mused, or Delicious Dark Coral? Cool Caramel?

"I've got one called 'Temptress Treat'", commented Julia, coming into Lucy's room. "That might do the trick with Tristan."

"Don't make me laugh," giggled Lucy. "I haven't got

time to laugh. I should have gone by now; you know what those buses are like. Oh, who's that at the door? Tell them to go away, whoever it is!"

"Yes Milady," answered Julia solemnly. "Of course Milady, anything you say, Milady; allow me to open the door for you."

Julia dashed downstairs and flung open the door to reveal a very tired and dishevelled looking Steve.

"Hi!" he said. "You must be Julia. I'm Steve, Steve from choir."

"Hello," squeaked Julia, overcome by the apparition before her. Crikey, he's so gorgeous, she thought. Why on earth is Lucy chasing Tristan when there are hunks like this in the choir?

"Is Lucy still here?" asked Steve. "I was just passing and thought she might like a lift to choir, considering how wet it is."

"Yes, she's in and yes, it is so wet, I mean, oh, come in, you're getting soaked," said Julia. "I'll tell Lucy you're here."

"I won't come in," said Steve. "I'll wait here, if you could ask her if she wants a lift."

"Of course," said Julia and bounded up the stairs, two at a time

"Well, what a good looking man. Is he attached? Is he interested in women? What's the story?"

"What are you talking about, Julia," asked a very perplexed Lucy.

"Why, Steve, of course," answered Julia. "He's downstairs waiting for you and wants to give you a lift to choir. He says he's on his way there now and thought you might like a lift because of the rain."

"But it's totally out of his way," frowned Lucy.

"So he's got another reason; who cares? Just go down and be nice to him," urged Julia. "He's obviously keen on you, so slap on that lipstick. Come on now; don't keep a gorgeous bloke like that waiting!"

Julia hustled Lucy downstairs and out of the front door so fast that Lucy literally fell into Steve's arms.

"Steady," said Steve, very amused. "Shall we make a dash for the car? It's really pelting down now. Bye Julia!"

"Yes please," said Lucy, still amazed at the turn of events. "Bye Julia. See you later!"

"How was your weekend?" asked Lucy once they were in the car. "And how was your mother?" she added in a concerned tone.

"Thanks for asking," replied Steve. "She's bearing up and my dad is OK too."

Steve wished that Lucy showed signs of feeling something other than pity for him, but it was a start to feel something, he supposed.

"And how was your weekend? Did you enjoy your trip to Bath?"

"Oh yes," smiled Lucy, "I had a great time. I went to see my two nieces in their end of term ballet show; it was lovely and it was at the ballet school where I used to have lessons as a girl, the same teacher even, Mrs Doyle."

Steve swerved a little as a vision of Lucy in a skin tight leotard and pink tights and shoes popped into his mind.

"Oh, sorry," he answered. "I'm a bit tired. I'd better concentrate on the road."

"You look tired," said Lucy, concerned again.

Steve explained about the commuting he was doing and how he was trying to help his parents out the best he could.

"I owe it to them," he said simply. "They've always been there for me and I want to do what I can for them now. And how was your dinner with Tristan?" Steve continued casually, not wanting to appear too interested.

"Magical," breathed Lucy, "simply magical. He took me somewhere very special."

I bet he did, thought Steve grimly and he gripped the steering wheel so tightly he could see his knuckles standing out white against his hand. I'd like to thump him with these knuckles, thought Steve angrily. He's a complete and utter bastard, that's what he is.

Once they arrived at choir, Lucy dashed off to find Deborah, so that she could deliver Angela's message about being late.

"Thanks for letting me know, Lucy," said Deborah, making a note on her choir register. "But I hope Angela turns up soon, after all, she's only just joined the choir and it's not very professional, is it?"

"But we're not a professional choir, are we," said Lucy mischievously.

"No need for sarcasm," replied Deborah heavily.

"Well don't worry," said Lucy. "I've been giving Angela a bit of help with the notes and she's a fast learner."

"You," gasped Deborah in surprise. "How could you help Angela with the notes?"

"I can read music, you know," snapped Lucy defensively. "And I can play the piano."

Oh, what's the use, thought Lucy. I don't know why I'm bothering to defend Angela. Deborah doesn't understand; people like her never do.

Just then, Angela bounded up to Deborah and Lucy.

"I'm here! Isn't it great! Jeffrey got home sooner than he thought and I got a taxi to get here as soon as possible.

"You said Angela was going to be late," Deborah hissed to Lucy.

"Yes, she was, I mean she might have been, it was just in case. Oh, this is pointless; I'm going to sit down."

Lucy hurried to the front row where the seats were going fast but she was too late and had to take her place in the second row behind Claire.

"Yes," Claire was confiding to her neighbour, "the Castle Temple restaurant, way out in the country, on Sunday evening."

Lucy was straining to hear now. What was Claire talking about?

"He's taken me there once before," continued Claire, "but I slapped his face then."

Clare and her neighbour broke into fits of giggles at this point.

"No need to give in too early, is there? Anyway, we had a great weekend and I mean really great!"

Another of her conquests, thought Lucy disparagingly. Perhaps she'll leave Tristan alone now. But what a coincidence going to the Castle Temple restaurant - exactly where Tristan took me on Friday. Lucy shifted in her seat and felt a bit uneasy then she lit up at the sight of Tristan as he swept into the room, curls flying.

"Good evening ladies and gentlemen and what a lovely one it is too! Let's get this show on the road."

"He's in a good mood," remarked Steve's neighbour in the basses.

"New conquest, so the gossip goes," remarked another bass. "He's been after her for ages and finally got her, if you get my drift, this past weekend. She's one of the sopranos, don't know which one, but we'll soon find out in the pub afterwards no doubt."

Steve stared at his music miserably. Pleases God, no, no, it can't be, he thought. I don't believe it, don't want to believe it. Tristan and Lucy? It's not possible. Steve lifted his head up to look across the rows of basses in front of him, over to the far side of the piano where Lucy sat in the sopranos. She smiled at him and gave a little half wave, then lifted her music quickly as Tristan's voice boomed out.

"A week on Saturday, ladies and gentlemen, that's when this concert is! You're not ready yet but I'm here to change all that! Now, full steam ahead: let's get on with it! From the top, Miss Greymitt, from the top. All stand!"

Tristan seems so dynamic this evening, thought Lucy. I wonder what's got into him? It must be the adrenaline flowing as the concert's so close. He's magnificent!

Claire smirked in the front row, delighted at Tristan's

energy. She glanced down at her hands and frowned slightly as she noticed that she'd broken a nail. Really, her hands were looking very rough with all the extra housework she was doing for Tristan.

As planned, Claire had taken today off work, knowing that Tristan would be busy in London. She had let herself into his house with the spare key she had taken from his cellar and had spent the day cleaning and scrubbing his kitchen and bathroom until they positively gleamed.

Tristan will have such a surprise when he goes home tonight, Claire thought in amusement. He has no idea what will be waiting for him and I don't just mean the clean bathroom and kitchen! Claire had put a bottle of champagne in the fridge and was planning to go back to Tristan's house after choir and wait for him there. She smiled secretively to herself and missed the next soprano entry.

"Come on," urged Deborah, the soprano voice representative. "Come on Claire! Concentrate! Don't let the sopranos down! We've got the concert soon."

"Sorry," mouthed Claire. "I was miles away."

I wish I was miles away, thought Claire dreamily and I wish Deborah would get off my back. She's such a prig.

Claire suddenly put her fingers in her ear and leaned away from Deborah slightly, frowning.

"Oh, sorry, Deborah," Claire apologised. "It's just that I find it difficult to get my note when you're singing so loudly and actually, you know, you are a teensy bit flat this evening and it's ever so slightly off putting to the rest of us, you know."

Several sopranos sitting around Claire and Deborah smirked at this exchange and one even started to say that she had wondered who it had been, singing quite so flat. Deborah coloured and became engrossed in her Belshazzar score.

"What a bitch that Claire is," whispered Angela to Lucy. "Can you believe she spoke to Deborah like that?"

Before Lucy could reply, Tristan roared out

"What is going on in the soprano section? Don't you ladies understand how little time we've got? Now belt up and get on with it!"

Miss Greymitt winced as she played, shocked to hear Tristan speaking to the ladies of the choir in such tones. It was never like this in the days of Sir Digby Fork, Tristan's illustrious predecessor, who had set up the choir many years ago and trained Tristan up as his protégé. Poor Sir Digby had passed on now, but think how appalled he would have been, thought Miss Greymitt with a shudder. Dear Sir Digby, he was always the perfect gentleman and she herself had been so very young then and…

"Miss Greymitt!" roared Tristan. "What the hell are you playing? This isn't "Listen with Mother", you know; this is serious stuff! Let me show you how to do your job. Here, get off the piano stool."

"Steady on Tristan, old chap," said the chairman of the choir, jumping up from the tenors and rushing over to Miss Greymitt's defence. "Steady on now. I'm sure we should all be concentrating more but we need a break; it's way over the usual time for our break."

"You're not having a break," shouted Tristan, stamping his foot.

"Yes we are," said the chairman firmly. "Break time everyone! Make it short because we've plenty of work to do."

The chairman sighed and rolled his eyes at Miss Greymitt with a sympathetic smile. Tristan was always like this before a concert, in fact he was usually much worse. They were escaping lightly this time.

Claire rushed over to Tristan and put her arm round him protectively.

"Tristan darling," she gushed. "It'll be all right! We didn't mean to annoy you!"

A particularly sharp-eyed bass noticed Claire's concern and put two and two together. By the end of the coffee break, most of the basses were looking at Claire with renewed interest and Steve was grinning from ear to ear.

"Sorry for my outburst, ladies and gentlemen," said Tristan by way of apology, "and I must apologise to you, Miss Greymitt, especially. The artistic temperament, you know. Beyond my control!"

Miss Greymitt nodded her acceptance of Tristan's apology and the rehearsal proceeded briskly. Deborah wondered why Tristan thought that he was a better musician because he had no self control. Angela speculated with amusement that if her daughter Amy had stamped her feet and shouted like Tristan, she would have had time out in her bedroom and possibly even no television for the rest of the day.

At the end of the rehearsal, Claire made her way over to Tristan.

"Darling, I've such a headache! I'm going straight home, but you go to the pub, go and have a quiet drink then you can give me a ring later in the week…yes, that would be lovely; I'll speak to you tomorrow then."

Tristan looked at Claire's retreating figure. That's very strange, he thought. I was sure she'd want to come to the pub with me. Oh, never mind. Perhaps I can try my luck with Lucy. Tristan licked his lips with relish.

"Going to the pub, Lucy?" asked Steve, coming up to Lucy.

"No, yes, that is, I mean," began Lucy.

"Oh, by the way," whispered Steve. "Tristan has a new conquest, apparently. It's Claire!"

"No!" gasped Lucy in surprise. "No!' she repeated. "Not Claire! Of course it isn't her."

What was going on, Lucy wondered. Perhaps someone had started a silly rumour. How typical, she thought. People love a bit of scandal and what they don't know, they make up.

"No," said Lucy again. "Claire isn't his latest conquest, why, she's gone home. She's not interested in Tristan."

"Listen Lucy," said Steve urgently. "Don't let Tristan make a fool of you. He's no good. He treats women like dirt and you should steer well clear of him."

"Why I do believe you're jealous, Steve," teased Lucy, her head on one side.

"Oh, grow up Lucy," hissed Steve, his temper flaring. "I'm saying these things for your own good but you're too obsessed to listen. I'm off home. I've got sixth form essays I should mark and I need some sleep. Can I give you a lift? No? Then I'll say goodnight."

Lucy stared after Steve in astonishment. What did I say, she wondered. Oh well, off to the pub I think. She hurried out of the hall and bumped straight into Tristan, who was lying in wait for her.

"Lucy," he drawled. "So good to see you!"

"Oh Tristan," exclaimed Lucy, "thank you so much for dinner last Friday. I really loved the restaurant."

"How about the company," leered Tristan, putting his face close to hers.

"That too," laughed Lucy nervously.

"Fancy a drink?" asked Tristan. "I know a little wine bar near here where we won't be disturbed."

"Don't you want to go to the pub," said Lucy, "I mean with the others?"

"Nope," answered Tristan, with a toss of his curls, "Do you?"

"Nope," laughed Lucy.

"Come on then." Tristan took her arm and hurried her away through the gloomy cold streets at such a rate that Lucy felt quite bewildered.

"Tristan! I don't even know where I am," said Lucy breathlessly, then Tristan suddenly pushed her through the doorway of a wine bar, ordered a bottle of his usual and pulled her over to a corner table.

Lucy giggled. "This is all very secretive," she whispered. "What's going on?"

"I'm crazy about you," sighed Tristan, raising his glass

to her, "and I think you're crazy about me."

Lucy giggled again.

"I suppose so," she said. "I admire you so much, I mean for your music."

"Is that all?" purred Tristan, putting his arm round Lucy. "Come on, have another glass, that's it; it's just like fruit juice really."

Goodness, thought Lucy, I feel so dizzy. It seems a long time since the shepherd's pie at Angela's house.

"Do they have food here?" she ventured. "Just a snack or something? I am a bit hungry."

"No, no food, they don't do food. You'd better come home with me and I'll cook you an omelette. Come on now; finish your drink."

"But I'm sure I saw someone eating toast and pate up at the bar," slurred Lucy. "Look, there's a blackboard with a menu on, over there by the door."

"It's finished," said Tristan firmly. "No food after 9pm. I know this place. Come on; my car's very near and we can take the rest of the bottle with us."

Still protesting, Lucy was ushered out of the door and before she knew it, she was sinking into Tristan's leather car upholstery, being driven through Springfield at breakneck speed.

"I should go home," she said sleepily. "I've got a rehearsal for the school carol service in the morning at school."

"You'll be fine, sweetie," soothed Tristan. "Get out of my way, you cretin," he suddenly snarled. "No, not you, sweetie, it's that moron in the Skoda in front of us."

That same evening, Claire had arrived at Tristan's house soon after choir and had begun to put her plan into action. First she ran herself a bath and had a good long soak in perfumed oil, then she put on her new red négligée and hopped into Tristan's bed to await his arrival.

"I do hope he isn't long," Claire had yawned, stretching out, then curling into a ball again. "I'll just have a little doze for a few minutes."

Claire was so exhausted from all her cleaning and scrubbing that she soon dropped off to sleep and so didn't hear Tristan and Lucy arrive.

"Come in, sweetie," said Tristan to Lucy. "Come into the kitchen and let's have that omelette."

Lucy looked about her in surprise. She wouldn't have thought a bachelor could be so house proud. The kitchen was absolutely spotless.

Tristan was surprised too. Did I clean up this morning, he wondered vaguely. The house has been looking a lot tidier this week, I must say and it smells nice in here. I didn't know I'd emptied the rubbish bin, after all, it's only Wednesday and I usually do that on Saturday.

"Sit down," ordered Tristan , indicating a chair. "I won't be a minute; I'll just find the eggs."

When Tristan opened the fridge, he saw the champagne and also noticed that there were all sorts of interesting delicacies waiting to be eaten. Perhaps Claire brought them round on Sunday, he thought. That's it; I must have not noticed earlier in the week. All very convenient, I must say.

"Champagne?" Tristan suggested, brandishing the bottle.

"No, no Tristan, I really shouldn't; I've had far too much to drink already. Oh! What was that noise?"

"I didn't hear anything," leered Tristan. "Come here gorgeous."

"No, certainly not, no Tristan, that is, oh I think I'll just go to the loo if you don't mind. Is it upstairs?"

"Straight upstairs and at the end of the landing; it's the door in the middle," answered Tristan. "Don't be long now," he added, as he pulled the champagne cork out with a satisfying pop.

Lucy made her escape upstairs and found the bathroom.

"Goodness, it's so clean in here," she declared.

"Tristan is amazing!"

While Lucy was in the bathroom, Claire woke up and looked out of the window to see if Tristan's car was there. Great, she thought when she saw his Porsche. Not long now. I'll just snuggle down in bed. Tristan's going to have such a surprise!

Tristan loaded some food and champagne onto a tray, just as Claire had done for him at the weekend and made his way upstairs.

"Ready or not, here I come darling!" he called.

"Bother," said Claire. "He knows I'm here. Never mind; it'll still be fun."

Lucy emerged from the bathroom to be faced with an ardent Tristan with his tray full of goodies. He quickly set the tray down on the floor and swept Lucy into his arms.

"You're so light," he marvelled. "Like a little bird."

"No Tristan," said Lucy, struggling. "No, not now, not like this."

"Yes", said Tristan, pushing open his bedroom door with his foot and carrying Lucy to the bed, her hair trailing in a red silken mass over his arm.

"Oh Tristan," murmured Lucy.

"Oh Tristan!" shouted Claire in fury, standing on the bed now, quivering with anger, her raven hair flowing down her back. "I always knew you were a rat, but this takes the biscuit, you complete bastard!"

"Oh my God," yelled Tristan, secretly thinking that Claire looked absolutely terrific in her satin négligée with her dark eyes flashing. He wondered briefly if perhaps both these lovely women would be interested in… but no; one glance at Lucy's tear stained face told him that only one course of action remained available to him.

"I'm sorry," Tristan mumbled as he fled down the stairs two at a time, ran out of the house and sped away in his car. "I'm so sorry my darlings."

Chapter Nine:
Howl ye, howl ye, therefore

Steve felt wretched the next morning as he remembered his quarrel with Lucy. I shouldn't have been so blunt, he thought; I just didn't know how to warn her about Tristan, particularly after hearing the gossip about him and Claire at choir. Perhaps I should ring her this evening, he wondered. I want to make sure she still comes to the party on Saturday. I do hope I haven't put her off. Yes, that's what I'll do; I'll ring her this evening.

Steve smiled and began gathering up his exercise books and notes in the staff room, ready to set off for his first lesson of the day.

"Everything OK?" asked Hermione Trubshaw, Steve's Head of Department, in a concerned but cheerful voice.

"Going to be, I think," answered Steve. "Definitely going to be."

Steve's lesson with Year 9 went like clockwork, as usual. He had taught this group since they were Year 7s and had got them working just the way he wanted now. Steve surveyed the rows of bent heads in front of him, feverishly scribbling away as they completed their end of term test for him, all anxious to do their best. A sudden shaft of winter sun beamed through the window and Steve was reminded of the rich colour of Lucy's hair. Stop it, said Steve to himself sternly. I must concentrate on the task in hand.

"Five more minutes," he warned the bent heads. "Don't forget to read your answers through carefully and check your spelling and punctuation please. You don't get any marks if I can't understand what you're saying."

Steve wondered what state his parents would be in this evening. He hadn't been with them last night because of choir, but had left food ready for them. He was going to try to nip off early this afternoon and hopefully get to them before the rush hour. Steve was just beginning to plan what sort of provisions he could pick up at the village shop on the way to his parents' cottage, when he became aware that the test should have finished by now and that several pupils were getting restless.

"Stop writing now," he said quickly. "Yes, even you, Henry. Now, who would like to collect the tests in? Caroline? Thank you. No, it doesn't matter what order they're in; just a neat pile. Thanks."

I've never been so distracted in a lesson, thought Steve. I've got to get a grip.

"Everything all right, sir?" enquired Caroline. "You look tired sir, if you don't mind me saying so."

"I do mind," said Steve gently, as several of the boys sniggered. "No personal remarks Caroline, we agreed. Do you remember?"

"Sorry sir," spluttered Caroline, bright red. She had quite a crush on Steve and had already been taken aside by Hermione Trubshaw, for a little talk about it. Steve sighed. He might have to talk to Hermione about it again. It would come better from a woman, he supposed. He had found girls getting crushes on him to be an occupational hazard of teaching. He was young, single and good looking and it seemed inevitable that some girls would be fascinated by him. Hermione had often told him to be careful,

"Because as a man, Steve, you can have absolutely no idea how foolish and excitable teenage girls can be."

Steve had replied that he had a fair idea, after all he did have two older sisters and had spent hours of his childhood listening to them discussing which of their teachers were hunks and which were complete nerds.

Steve packed the Year 9 tests into his bag as he dismissed the class.

"Good morning Sir and thank you," they chanted and then streamed out of the class on their way to PE.

"Quietly!" warned Steve, then sat down for a few minutes before the arrival of his next class. He could probably mark the tests at lunchtime if he didn't eat anything much, or perhaps he should take them back to his parents' cottage? Steve groaned and put his head in his hands. He felt one of his familiar headaches creeping up on him and wondered if he should take a migraine tablet.

"Morning Mr Goodman," said a cheery sixth former, coming in for his A'level lesson.

"Have you marked our work yet, Sir?" remarked another pupil. "I'm hoping for at least a B, or me mum'll be annoyed. She says I should be getting higher grades. She thinks I'm lazy!"

"Yes," smiled Steve. "I've marked your essays. I finished them last night, or was it early this morning? Anyway, I've done them. Are the others on their way? Good. We can make a start then. I'd like to talk to you all individually about your essays, which were of course brilliant. Yes, Tom, particularly yours! Now, sit down. I've got some photocopied articles for you to read and discuss and I'll see you at my desk one at a time while the rest of you read the articles. Oh good, hurry up you lot and sit down; we all seem to be here now. Well, Tom, you'd better come up and have a look at your essay with me. Yes, don't worry, your mum's definitely going to be pleased with you this week. That's your first A this term, isn't it? Well done! Now, just a few points…"

I really love teaching the sixth form, Steve thought. I can sense real enthusiasm coming from this group in particular and I wouldn't be surprised if quite a few of them went on to study history or a related subject at degree level. Teaching's not such a bad job, thought Steve in satisfaction and even his headache started to ebb away towards the end of the double lesson.

Lucy had a truly fearsome headache that morning as she rehearsed for the school Carol Concert.

"Sing up!" she yelled at her Year 7s and 8s. "Oh sing up can't you and stop talking! I can't hear the descant at all."

Lucy ran her fingers over her puffy, swollen eyes. She didn't know how she had managed to get to school this morning; it all seemed like some sort of nightmare.

"I won't think about it now, I won't," she snarled fiercely through her teeth. "I've got to get on with this rehearsal."

"First sign of madness," remarked one of the cheeky Year 7 boys.

"Oh be quiet!" shouted Lucy over the din. "Let's go from the second verse of "In the bleak midwinter". Now, do your best, because Mrs Goodshoe is coming to the rehearsal in ten minutes time to listen to you perform."

And is she going to be disappointed, thought Lucy. These kids can't sing for toffee and it's not my fault. Oh, my head! I'm dying for a coffee.

"In the bleak midwinter," roared the children, "Frosty wind made mooooan!"

"Earth stood hard as ironing," continued one joker as a solo and then fell suddenly silent as Mary Goodshoe entered the hall, plodding heavily in her beige lace up shoes, her navy pleated skirt swinging from side to side. She took one look at Lucy's ashen face, frowned at the disorderly rabble masquerading as the Junior Choir and acted immediately.

"Sit down children, yes, I mean now Ben. If I hear a sound from you, from anyone, it's detention time. Miss Lavender, may I have a word?"

Mary hustled Lucy out of the door and the children all leaned forwards in their chairs to try to hear what the two teachers were saying. They could see Mrs Goodshoe through the glass door putting a sympathetic hand on Lucy's shoulder.

"Cor," remarked Jason. "That Miss Lavender, she's crying."

"Is not," retorted Jane.

"Maybe not," ventured Oliver, "but she doesn't look well, does she?"

"We shouldn't have been playing up, should we?"

"No."

"Oh come on. She was asking for it."

Suddenly Mrs Goodshoe stared through the glass door and a deadly silence fell over the children again.

"You mean you didn't get any sleep at all?" Mary asked Lucy incredulously. "You poor love. Now go to the staff room and have a coffee. I'll take over here and let's see how you feel after lunch."

Lucy stumbled blindly to the staff room and made herself a strong coffee. After a few chocolate biscuits she began to feel better and also to feel angry.

Why, Tristan is such a coward, she thought. He could at least have stayed around to face the music. I mean, what was he thinking of? I still don't understand what was going on last night.

Lucy was furious that after a heated exchange with Claire, during which Claire had called Lucy a "frigid little milksop" and Lucy had likened Claire to a "bitch on heat," Lucy had been forced to make her own way back home.

She had fled out of Tristan's house in a terrible state, leaving the front door wide open, then sneaked back in to get her bag which she had left in the kitchen, terrified that she might bump into Claire again. Lucy couldn't be sure, but she thought she had heard Claire laughing upstairs. The woman is obviously completely mad, Lucy had thought. Fancy breaking into someone's house and waiting for him in bed when there has been no encouragement! I suppose she's desperate, Lucy had thought as she had made her way down the hill to the main road and had waited in vain for a taxi to pass by. Perhaps she is a nymphomaniac and she's been stalking Tristan.

After waiting for ages, Lucy had decided to walk to the local train station to see if she could ring for a taxi from there. As she had stumbled along the road, totally exhausted, her salvation had appeared in the form of the night bus. Flagging it down, Lucy had sobbed with relief and spent the entire journey home slumped in her seat crying.

"You all right, love?" the driver had asked in a gruff voice. "Man trouble, innit?"

Lucy preferred not to think about the rest of the night, how she had sobbed and cried and fretted for what seemed like hours. Julia, although in a deep sleep fuelled by rather too much wine, had eventually been roused and had sat with Lucy until the early hours of the morning, making her tea and hugging her.

"You see," Julia had said forcefully, "Tristan is a rat. You'll believe it now."

"But Julia," Lucy had sobbed. "I honestly don't think he realised she was there. I mean, he looked as shocked as I was. She was just throwing herself at him. It's disgusting! Poor Tristan."

Mulling it over in the staff room with a cup of coffee, Lucy knew that Tristan was at fault too. He shouldn't have run away. He should have got rid of Claire, that's what he should have done. Lucy smiled a sad smile as she realised that the man she idolised was a coward and had feet of clay. I wonder where he went last night, mused Lucy. He must have felt terrible as well.

She would never in a million years have guessed at the truth, have guessed that her Tristan had sneaked back to his house after an hour, hoping that the coast would be clear and that he could have a stiff drink and go bed. Tristan had been amazed and delighted to find that Claire was still there, waiting for him.

"I thought I'd blown it with you, my darling," he had murmured, taking her in his arms.

"You don't get rid of me that easily," Claire had whispered in return. "But try a stunt like that again and I promise you, you'll regret it."

"Why?" Tristan had asked in sudden interest. "What will you do?"

"Well…" Claire had begun.

"Oh Claire," Tristan had whispered later. "You're quite a woman."

While Lucy was feeling angry over her coffee in the staff room, Tristan and Claire were still frolicking in bed.

"Don't you ever do that again, Tristan," warned Claire. "I mean it."

"Promise," sighed Tristan happily. "You're enough for me."

Claire was enough of a realist to know that Tristan would almost definitely try it again, if not with Lucy then with someone else, but she had set her heart and mind on Tristan and had decided to accept him, warts and all. And maybe the warts will fade with time, she thought happily; anyway, it's too late. I've burned my boats so he's stuck with me.

"You don't think I ought to phone Lucy, do you?" asked Tristan guiltily. "I mean, she did look upset, didn't she?"

"She'll get over it," laughed Claire. "And so will you."

But Tristan had enough that was decent in him to realise that he'd better contact Lucy later to make sure she had got home safely and was all right. He'd ring her this evening when he got home from school, that's what he'd do.

In the afternoon, Claire decided she had better show her face at work; after all, she had taken a day off on Wednesday to clean Tristan's house and this morning she had used the excuse of a migraine. Her colleagues had been surprised to see her looking quite so radiant when she waltzed into the office on Thursday afternoon, cheeks glowing and eyes sparkling delightfully.

"I wish we could all have headaches like you," said one of her colleagues enviously.

"Yes, he is rather delicious," answered Claire dreamily. "Oh, quick, here's the boss! I'd better get down to some work."

"Feeling better?" Claire's boss had asked vaguely.

"That's good," he added as he wandered off.

"You get away with it every time," complained Claire's colleague crossly. "One day you'll get caught out, mark my words."

Claire smiled enigmatically.

"I hope so," she said simply. "That is the plan, anyway."

Lucy was still feeling so terrible in the afternoon that Mary Goodshoe took pity on her and sent her home. But Lucy didn't go home. She still felt furious with Tristan and what she felt for Claire was more akin to hatred. She decided to go round to Tristan's house to have it out with him, to ask him why he had abandoned her in such a humiliating situation. She was surprised at her own boldness, but utterly determined to confront Tristan.

As Lucy crunched across the gravel to Tristan's front door, she noticed the glass in the porch sparkling and the brass door knocker winking at her in the bright winter sun. Again, she was impressed that Tristan was so house proud. I would never have thought he had it in him, Lucy marvelled, so perhaps I have misjudged him in other ways as well.

She rang the door bell. When Tristan answered the door and Lucy saw how desperately tired and almost guilty he looked, her heart turned over and she wanted to make everything all right for him.

"Lucy!" exclaimed Tristan in amazement. "I thought you'd never want to see me again. Are you OK? Did you get home all right? Well, you obviously did; what a silly question. Oh, come in, won't you? Come in and tell me you're not angry with me."

"I'm not angry any more," said Lucy primly, "but I'm so disappointed."

Tristan did his best to look ashamed.

"I mean, Tristan, why did you run away? You should have stayed to face the music, in a manner of speaking…"

Lucy's voice trailed off as she realised that Tristan seemed relieved and even amused.

"Tristan!" shouted Lucy. "You just can't behave like that! What were you thinking of? You left me and I had to get home on my own in the middle of the night!"

Lucy burst into noisy tears and Tristan folded her in his arms.

"Oh, Lucy, Oh Lucy darling, I'm so sorry, I'm such a coward you see; it was just that I couldn't face you both at once."

"But why was Claire in your bedroom?" asked Lucy with a sniff. "Is she stalking you? Oh Tristan, why didn't you tell me about it?"

"Well, it's not really like that," began Tristan, then said hastily after a quick look at Lucy's face, "but yes, of course, she has been simply throwing herself at me; of course I never ever encouraged her. Oh, Lucy, please don't cry."

Tristan patted Lucy's back absentmindedly and wondered how he was going to get out of this one. Perhaps Lucy would give up on him now and maybe that would be for the best, after all, he had Claire now and yet, and yet… Tristan looked down at Lucy's fragile shoulders, heaving with emotion and longed to sweep her off her feet and carry her upstairs to bed. No, he thought sternly to himself. It's not fair; I must discourage her, but gently.

"Lucy," he began, "Lucy my love, I'm not worthy of you. It's for the best if we don't meet up like this again. It's over between us, really it is. I'm no good for you."

"Oh Tristan," interrupted Lucy passionately. "Don't ever say you're not worthy of me. You're such a wonderful talented person, but I still can't understand what happened. I suppose you didn't want to hurt anyone's feelings so you just ran away. Is that what happened? Is it?"

Lucy's voice trailed off doubtfully while Tristan continued to pat her back.

"Let's forget all about it, Tristan," said Lucy brightly.

"Let's put it behind us and forget all about that Claire. She's so obvious; I mean, why would you be interested in her? She needs to see a psychiatrist, stalking you like that. I almost feel sorry for her. Anyway, I'm off now. I need to get some sleep. Don't forget the party at Grangewood Golf Club on Saturday. I've got you a ticket. Here it is; I'll leave it on the hall table where you'll notice it. I'll meet you there."

And with that, Lucy was gone, running as fast as she could down the hill to catch a bus home.

"Grangewood Golf Club?" said Tristan aloud. "Whatever is she going on about? Wait a minute. I seem to remember she said something about going to a party with her before. Oh well, I wonder when it is?"

As Tristan closed the front door, the draught blew the ticket for the party up into the air and then it floated gently down to the floor to lie undiscovered for a time under the hall table.

Could do with some sleep myself, thought Tristan with a yawn and a stretch, and he made his way upstairs to his bedroom where the bed was still unmade from the morning's activities. Tristan smiled and lay down on the bed with his clothes and his shoes still on. He was asleep within minutes.

Lucy's hopeful mood had faded by the next day and she had to concentrate hard to get through her lessons and rehearsals for the school Carol Concert. Still, it's Friday, she kept telling herself and tomorrow it's the party. Her flatmate Julia was amazed that Lucy was still contemplating going to the party with Tristan.

"You must be crazy," she said to Lucy on Friday evening after school in their flat. "Out of your skull, mad, deluded."

"Don't spare my feelings, will you," laughed Lucy. "I mean, say what you really feel, why don't you?"

"I'm sorry Lucy," continued Julia sternly, "But that

man is a complete rat and I can't for the life of me understand your fascination with him. Especially when there are men like Steve around."

Julia had even thought in a vague sort of way of having a crack at Steve herself, but she knew he wouldn't be interested in her and to be honest he wasn't really her type either. Julia sighed. She never seemed to be able to find anyone who could hold her interest for more than a few weeks.

"Men," she said contemptuously. "Who needs them?"

Lucy and Julia both started giggling.

"Come on," said Julia. "Let's go out this evening, just the two of us. We could go and see a film or something. What about it?"

"Why not?" said Lucy. "And I promise not to mention Tristan's name!"

The two of them had a fun evening together, watching a romantic film (during which Lucy shed a few tears) and then going out for a pizza.

"Lucy," began Julia over the pizza. "I know we said we wouldn't mention Tristan's name, but has it ever occurred to you that he is actually carrying on with Claire and that far from throwing herself at him, he's been chasing her and is stupid or conceited enough to think that he's still entitled to chase you as well?"

"No, no, absolutely not," replied Lucy firmly. "If I ever thought that Tristan would do that, well, that would be it forever I'm afraid. No, Julia, it isn't possible; he's explained it all to me and I believe him. He knows he shouldn't have run away. That was his only mistake."

"Well, have it your own way," warned Julia darkly, "But I think you're deluding yourself. Anyway, let's go home. We need our beauty sleep because it's the party tomorrow!"

"And we haven't decided what to wear yet," laughed Lucy. "Come on. Let's go home."

As Julia and Lucy made their way back to their flat, Claire was letting herself into Tristan's house with her borrowed key. She noticed the scrap of paper under the hall table straight away.

"What's that?" she hissed in annoyance. "Tristan is so untidy; doesn't he know what rubbish bins are for?"

Claire picked the ticket up and scrutinised it.

"Grangewood Golf Club Party. Saturday 2nd December," she read. "7.30 pm to midnight. Music from the Blue Sunset Band. Proceeds to the Springfield Teachers' Association."

"Teachers?" wondered Claire aloud. "Teachers?"

Oh, that milksop Lucy must have left this for Tristan when she was here on Wednesday. Really, she is pathetic. As if he'd want to go to a party with a bunch of teachers! I wonder if they wear mortar boards when they dance, thought Claire with a giggle. She had no time for teachers or schools and was proud of the fact that she had been expelled from her convent school at the age of sixteen for smoking and flirting with the gardener. If only the nuns had known, thought Claire in amusement. Flirting indeed! She tore the ticket into tiny pieces with great satisfaction and then threw them into the rubbish bin. I've got other plans for Saturday night, thought Claire with a smirk.

Chapter Ten: They drank wine again

IT was five o'clock on Saturday and the musicians from the Blue Sunset Band were beginning to arrive at Grangewood Golf Club.

"Better get set up and run through a couple of numbers," said Dan, the leader of the band. "Where's Trevor? He promised he wouldn't be late today. Here, I'll help you with that."

Dan helped Pete the drummer assemble his kit and then lifted his own saxophone out of its case and tried a few runs and solos.

"Phew!" he protested, wiping his brow. "I'm puffed already! Better have a fag and a cup of tea to settle me. Can't take the late nights like I used to, eh!"

"There's life in the old dog yet!" answered Pete, grinning broadly, but he too was feeling rather jaded. He moved awkwardly at his drums. Why were leather trousers so uncomfortable, he wondered. This pair seemed to have shrunk. He stood up and stretched.

"Ah! That's better," he said. "Yeah, thanks for the tea, Dan, mate. Oh, here's Trevor. Come on, mate; we're having a brew."

"Yes, come on Trevor. Don't you need to try the piano?" asked Dan.

"I got here as fast as I could," said Trevor primly, recoiling in sudden horror as he noticed Pete's leather trousers. "As you know, I have my teaching on Saturdays and I was asked to play for some dance classes at short notice."

Pete did a pirouette and fell heavily to the floor, laughing coarsely.

"What's that?" asked Trevor petulantly.

"Nothing," answered Dan. "You're here now. That's all that matters. And here are Chris and Tony. Good, we can make a start."

What a shambles, thought Dan in despair. He'd always

had trouble finding a keyboard player for this group and he didn't see Trevor staying for long. He just didn't fit in, that was the trouble, although there was no denying that he knew his stuff. Dan listened in grudging admiration as Trevor ran his long, immaculately manicured fingers over the ivories. If Trevor would loosen up a little and the others would stop teasing him, they might get somewhere.

"Come on you two," Dan said to Chris and Tony. "We haven't got all day."

Chris hastily tuned his bass guitar and Tony started making terrible breathy squawking noises.

"Need a new reed for this clarinet," Tony explained. "Wait a sec'. I know I've got one here. Soon be sorted out!"

Eventually the band got organised and began to make a decent sound.

"We'll try a few more numbers," said Dan. "Then off to the pub, I think, to prepare ourselves for the night ahead!"

"I hope the pub does bar snacks," commented Trevor. "I haven't had anything much to eat all day; I've been existing on Nice biscuits and tea."

Dan gave the others a look as he reassured Trevor.

"Don't worry. You can get something to eat in the pub but we are having a break around nine this evening and I've been told we're more than welcome to fill our faces at the buffet."

"Oh good," murmured Trevor in relief, although he doubted if he would be "filling his face" as Dan put it. He preferred picking daintily at his food, for he had a delicate stomach.

"Watch the old alcohol, boys," warned Dan. Pace yourselves through the evening if you can and no smoking while you're playing, Pete!"

"Yes," said Trevor. "Cigarette smoke plays havoc with my lungs. Asthma, you know," he continued. "A martyr to it since childhood."

"Fear not, Trevor, me old mate," laughed Pete. "I'm trying to give up anyway, so I'll do my best not to smoke over you."

"Should we get changed now, Dan?" Trevor asked. "I mean, before we go to the pub?"

"Good idea," said Dan. The band always played in dinner jackets and looked very smart. Pete was so relieved that he could change out of his uncomfortable leather trousers that he gave a whoop of glee and punched the air.

"Hey man," said Chris. "Save your energy."

"Yeah, stay cool," commented Tony.

The men changed quickly and then wandered off to the pub across the road to refresh themselves.

Lucy and Julia were refreshing themselves at home in Stanhope Gardens.

"Oh, this lipstick's gorgeous," shrieked Julia. "May I use it? Please Lucy?"

"Of course," giggled Lucy from the bathroom. "Help yourself to anything you want. I'll be raiding your dressing table in a minute, anyway."

Lucy had tried to ring Tristan to remind him about the party but his answer phone didn't seem to be working. She was thrilled to hear the sound of his voice, but soon realised it was his answer phone message.

"Hello! This is Tristan Proudfoot. I'm sorry I can't talk to you at the moment; I'm a little tied up but if you leave your name and number I'll get back to you."

Lucy tried to leave her message, but after hearing a click and a sound like someone breathing, the line went dead. She rang again, but the same thing happened.

How odd, Lucy had thought. Never mind. I know he'll remember, she had reassured herself. It will be different this time.

It wasn't until Lucy and Julia arrived at the golf club and had hung their coats up and admired themselves in the mirror that Lucy realised that she hadn't actually arranged with Tristan where to meet.

"Forget him," urged Julia. "Let's go and join in the fun and when he arrives, he'll find you."

Although it's more likely to be if he arrives, rather than when he arrives, thought Julia cynically.

"Come on Luce! Let's get a drink. Just listen to that music!"

"OK," agreed Lucy. "I suppose I don't need to wait at the door for him. He's not exactly lacking in confidence, after all. He's quite capable of walking into a room on his own, isn't he?"

Lucy and Julia made their way across the dance floor and over to the bar.

"Look!" said Julia in excitement. "There's your friend Steve over there and who is that hunk with him? Tell me I'm not dreaming! Is he single? Oh quick, Lucy. You've got to introduce me."

"That must be his friend Mark," said Lucy thoughtfully. "Steve has mentioned him a few times and said he was bringing him tonight."

"I think he's gorgeous," breathed Julia and Mark in his turn seemed to think Julia was equally gorgeous as he gazed admiringly in their direction.

Goodness, thought Lucy. Talk about eyes meeting across a crowded room.

Mark said something to Steve who then looked at Lucy and Julia and smiled. In no time at all, the four of them were chatting animatedly, straining to hear over the insistent beat of the music.

"Great band, don't you think?" Steve shouted in Lucy's ear.

She nodded in agreement.

"That Dan, the one playing saxophone at the moment, he's a friend of mine from college. He's a great bloke."

Lucy nodded again.

"Now," began Mark, "are you ladies going to stand by the bar all evening or would you like to dance?"

"Dance please," giggled Julia and Mark led her swiftly away.

"Looks like your friend Julia and my friend Mark are an item already," smiled Steve. Lucy nodded and turned to look at the door to see if Tristan had arrived.

"Would you like to dance, Lucy," asked Steve gently.

He knew that he had been a little heavy handed with Lucy after Wednesday's rehearsal, when he had warned her against Tristan and he had certainly been very bad tempered. But what a wonderful girl she is, thought Steve admiringly. She doesn't hold it against me at all.

"Would you like to dance, Lucy?" repeated Steve.

"Oh no, that is, I can't just now, maybe later," answered Lucy. "I'm waiting for my guest to arrive; he's a bit late."

"Your guest?" asked Steve in astonishment. "I thought you came with Julia!"

"Well of course I came with Julia," said Lucy. "After all, we do live at the same flat, but I bought an extra ticket and asked Tristan to come. Now I know you don't approve; you made your feelings perfectly clear on Wednesday but you are completely wrong about Tristan. All that gossip at choir is totally misplaced. Why, that Claire, she's just been throwing herself at Tristan and he's simply not interested."

Lucy broke off at this point and looked worried, as well she might. Even to her biased ears, the tale sounded unconvincing.

"Give up," urged Steve. "Give up on Tristan. He's no good. Whatever the truth about him and Claire, he's still not the right man for you."

"I'll wait a bit longer and make up my own mind," said Lucy icily.

Steve shook his head sorrowfully and made his way over to a group of colleagues. He noted that Miss Henshaw, the art teacher from his school was there, looking the picture of health. Funny how she's always ill during the week, thought Steve in amusement.

"Steve," said Susie Henshaw. "Thanks for covering for me last week when I was ill. I had terrible 'flu, you know."

"Actually," explained Steve, "I didn't cover for you. Mark took the lesson because I had rather a lot on."

"Oh, I didn't realise," said Susie, moving closer to Steve. "I do like your tie, Steve," she continued, reaching out to touch the silk.

"Thanks. Present from my sister," replied Steve. "I say, what about a dance, Susie? I really love this number."

The two of them made their way onto the dance floor as Lucy watched with a pang of regret. She stayed near the door for the next hour or so, chatting distractedly to anyone who came near.

Steve watched her growing more and more miserable as the evening progressed and was on the point of going over to her several times, but didn't want to annoy her. At nine o'clock, the band took a break and everyone descended on the buffet. Everyone that is, apart from Lucy, who made her way to the ladies and wept silently. I can't go home yet, she thought. He might still be coming - he might have had a puncture or something. I wish I had his mobile number; oh, I'm so miserable she sobbed. Lucy decided to ring Tristan's home number in case he was still there but when she tried there was no reply and the answer phone wasn't switched on.

Lucy made her way back to the party and went over to Julia.

"Hi Luce," smiled Julia. "I'm having a great time. Sorry if I've neglected you. Hey, what's wrong? Oh no, don't tell me Tristan isn't here yet?" she demanded.

Lucy nodded her head.

"Well, of all the nerve," began Julia. "And don't tell me you think there's a perfectly reasonable explanation for it. Come on, let's go and have something to eat. The queue's died down a bit now."

Steve was chatting to his friend Dan over a plate of food but he noticed that Lucy seemed to be OK and was eating with Julia.

"You see," explained Dan to Steve, "if only I could get the right mix of personalities, this band could really go places.

"You sound great to me," said Steve.

"Flatterer!" laughed Dan.

Trevor was tasting prawns daintily on the other side of the table while trying to move away from Pete's cigarette smoke.

"Pete!" Trevor whined. "You promised you wouldn't smoke near me."

"Sorry mate," replied Pete. "It's just that I'm gasping for a fag; it's been a long time since we were in the pub."

The band's break was soon over and they started playing a few gentle numbers while people finished eating. By ten o'clock the hall was really throbbing again as the rhythms pounded out.

Lucy decided to ring Tristan again although she knew in her heart there was no hope. This time the phone was answered straight away.

"I've been expecting you to ring," hissed Claire. "Too late, sweetie, that's all I can say. Too late!" Claire slammed the receiver down with a cackle.

"Who was that?" asked Tristan sleepily from the bed.

"No one," said Claire. "Absolutely no one."

Steve saw Lucy stumble back to the hall with red eyes and wondered what was going on. He went over to her and held out his hand.

"Have a dance with me, Lucy," Steve offered. "Please."

"I'd love to," answered Lucy simply and allowed Steve to lead her to the dance floor. He held her tight then whirled her round and round and on and on until they were both out of breath and laughing. Later on, during a slow number, Lucy whispered to Steve,

"I've been such a fool, you know, Steve. I feel like an idiot."

"You're not an idiot," grinned Steve. "Far from it."

Lucy sighed and relaxed her shoulders, snuggling closer to Steve.

"You're such a good friend, Steve," she whispered. "I know I can rely on you."

"I'll never let you down," murmured Steve. "Never."

Chapter Eleven: Yea, we wept

The next morning, Lucy and Julia were chatting over a very late breakfast.

"Well, you seemed to get on all right with Mark," teased Lucy.

"What about you and Steve?" asked Julia.

"Oh that," answered Lucy, suddenly embarrassed. "He must think I'm terrible, crying all over him just because Tristan didn't turn up."

"I hope you're not going to say there must be a good reason for Tristan's behaviour," said Julia sternly.

"Oh no," answered Lucy quickly. "I know the truth now, in fact I'm not sure what I saw in him. It's mad really, isn't it, how blind I've been."

"We all make mistakes," Julia reassured Lucy, giving her a hug. "It could happen to anyone."

"But it didn't happen to anyone," shouted Lucy angrily. "It happened to me and Steve knows all about it. He must think I'm a total idiot."

"Does it matter what other people think?" demanded Julia.

"Well," Lucy began, "actually I do mind what Steve thinks. He's proving to be a really good friend, you know."

"Yes," laughed Julia, "and he also happens to be six foot tall, good looking, kind and besotted with you."

"Oh no," said Lucy in a shocked voice. "It's nothing like that. He's just being friendly. He's so kind you know, why, you wouldn't believe all the things he was saying to me last night, saying that I could rely on him and, and…"

Julia raised one eyebrow and handed Lucy another cup of tea.

Later, when Lucy was getting dressed, the phone rang and she ran to the sitting room to answer it.

"Hello? Hello Lucy, it's Steve. I was wondering what you had planned for today and whether you'd like to meet up for lunch. You would? That's great. Perhaps lunch in a country pub? I can come straight over and collect you if you like. I'm at my flat in Springfield because it was too late to go back to my parents' cottage last night, so I'll come and pick you up in about twenty minutes, if that's all right with you? See you soon. Bye!"

"Twenty minutes!" shrieked Lucy. "I've only got twenty minutes!"

"What's going on?" asked Julia.

"Twenty minutes to get dressed," gasped Lucy. "It's Steve: he's taking me out for lunch in twenty minutes."

"But you are dressed, or nearly," laughed Julia.

"Yes, but I chose these clothes before I knew I was going out with Steve," reasoned Lucy. "Oh, help me, Julia! Quickly!"

"I think you should stay as you are," advised Julia firmly. "You look great but still relaxed and casual. Now calm down!"

Lucy rushed back to her bedroom and looked in the mirror. Her huge turquoise eyes stared back at her from a pale, rather tired looking face. Quick, blusher, thought Lucy and she hastily swept a tiny brush high over her cheeks and gave them a dusting of apricot. Now I look very tired with apricot blobs on my cheeks thought Lucy in a panic. I'll try the eyes. She carefully applied a thin green line under each eye and then smudged most of it off. Next she applied a large quantity of mascara to the upper lashes of one eye.

"Oh bother," she cried. "It's gone into a big clump!"

Lucy tried dabbing at her eye with some cotton wool and eye make up remover, but only succeeded in smearing the mascara over her contact lens.

"Oh no," moaned Lucy, as she ran to the bathroom. She put the plug in the basin and took out the lens, holding it delicately on her forefinger. She could see a great greasy smear of mascara on the surface of the lens. Breathing out with a large sigh, she sent the lens spinning through the air, on its way to an unknown location.

"Julia," screamed Lucy. "Don't come into the bathroom! You might tread on my lens."

"Whatever's the matter?" asked Julia, appearing at the bathroom door. "Oh! You've lost a lens again. Hold still Lucy; wait a minute."

Just then the doorbell rang.

"He's early!" shrieked a desperate Lucy. "He's early! He can't see me with only one lens in. Oh, help!"

"You mean you can't see him, surely?" asked Julia. "Anyway, stop panicking. I can see it on your jumper, look, there, right next to the cuff."

"Thank you Julia, thank you, thank you, thank you!" sobbed Lucy gratefully as she gently scooped up the lens, washed it quickly and put it back in her eye.

"I'll let Steve in and keep him chatting while you finish getting ready," said Julia with a smile and she disappeared downstairs to open the front door.

Lucy ran back to her bedroom and sprayed herself with a generous amount of Diorissima. She gazed at her face in the mirror, but it was difficult to see clearly because one eye was swimming with tears as she had only just put her lens in. Blinking hastily, she managed to clear the eye enough to finish applying her mascara to both eyes then she completed her look with a generous helping of orange coral lipstick.

Oh bother, thought Lucy. I've forgotten to use that new stuff under my eyes that's supposed to bounce the light away so that you don't look tired any more. Oh well, too late and it probably doesn't work anyway. I'll go and see him now.

Lucy found Steve in the sitting room, gazing at something on the mantelpiece.

"Lucy! How lovely to see you," said Steve warmly and he came straight over to her and kissed her on the cheek.

"Steve," whispered Lucy, suddenly embarrassed. "Where's Julia?"

"She's making us all some coffee," smiled Steve. "And

I've been looking at this picture on your mantelpiece, this picture of you. It's fabulous!"

"Oh that," said Lucy dismissively. "I'd forgotten all about that. A man drew my portrait on the train you know and then gave it to me."

"It's such a good likeness," said Steve in admiration, picking the drawing up carefully. "It's unmistakably you, but you're looking so sad."

"I was on my way back to London from my weekend in Bath with my sister. I suppose I didn't want to come back. In fact, I nearly didn't get on the train. I had a little fantasy about running away and never coming back to London."

"Poor Lucy," said Steve with genuine concern. "Hey, I've just noticed the signature. It's Nibbet, that's Robert Nibbet, isn't it?"

"Is it?" asked Lucy vaguely. "He seemed very nice. Is he famous?"

"Yes," said Steve excitedly. "He's well known, especially for his portraits. My parents have a couple of portraits of my sisters done by him when they were about four."

"But not one of you?" asked Lucy.

"Oh, I wasn't even born then," laughed Steve. "And I expect Robert Nibbet had got too expensive by the time I was four. He really is well known, you know."

"Goodness," said Lucy. "I ought to have taken more care of the drawing and not just dumped it on the mantelpiece."

Steve put the picture back gently as Julia came in. "It's so beautiful, don't you agree Julia?"

"I'm no judge," replied Julia, setting the tray down, "but yes, it does have something special about it. You should get it framed, Lucy."

"Maybe," said Lucy with a smile and Steve's heart turned over as he looked at her. He thought that it was not only the drawing that needed to be looked after and cherished.

At Tristan's house, Claire was preparing a large piece of beef to put in the oven. Tristan does love his meat so, Claire thought fondly as she put the roasting dish in the oven. She could hear Tristan pounding furiously at the piano in the music room as he bellowed,

"Then sing, sing aloud, sing aloud to God our strength."

"Make a joyful noise unto the God of Jacob," warbled Claire from the depths of the oven.

Oh bother, she thought. This oven still isn't clean. Claire had scrubbed away literally years of dirt during her spring-cleaning session but the oven had presented a particular challenge. Never mind, she thought happily. Tristan can buy me a new oven soon.

Just then, Tristan stuck his head round the kitchen door.

"Was I meant to be anywhere last night?" he demanded. "I have a vague feeling I was meant to be somewhere."

"No my darling," replied Claire. "You were exactly where you were supposed to be yesterday. Now, go back to your music, there's a dear. It's ages before lunch and I've got lots to do. Go on."

Tristan did as he was told, but as he walked through the hall, back to the music room, he remembered Lucy's visit after the fiasco and embarrassment of Wednesday evening. I was surprised she had the courage to come and see me, thought Tristan. I mean, I wouldn't have, if I'd been her, but she's an amazing girl. Suddenly Tristan remembered that he should have been at some party with Lucy last night, at a Golf Club or something, he thought.

"No," he groaned aloud. "How could I forget?" Then, with a guilty look at the kitchen door, he crept upstairs to the telephone in the bedroom. He looked Lucy's number up on his choir list, as it seemed to be completely illegible in his filofax, as if it had been scribbled over. He rang the number with some trepidation, carefully closing the bedroom door first.

"No, she isn't here," said Julia bluntly. "She's gone out for the day with an extremely nice young man. Don't bother to ring again."

Tristan sat on his bed, feeling sorry for himself. Now Lucy would never know how sorry he was and how bad he felt. He could do with a stiff drink. Down in the kitchen, Claire replaced the receiver on the kitchen phone with a smile of satisfaction. She had enjoyed listening to Tristan's phone call. That would be the end of that now.

After a quiet lunch in a country pub, Steve suggested a walk to Lucy.

"Oh yes," she smiled. "A walk would be lovely. Fresh air! That's what I need, to set me up for the week to come. It's my school concert next week, so I'll have a lot to do."

As they strolled along country lanes and looked out over wintry fields, Lucy relaxed and told Steve some of her worries about her teaching.

"It's not that I don't like the subject," she said with a laugh, "But I'm not sure I'm very good at making other people like it!"

"But you told me how much you enjoy teaching little Amy the piano," said Steve. "Classroom teaching isn't the only sort of teaching."

"Well," began Lucy, "I've often thought of giving up my school teaching and trying to see if I can make a living from piano teaching and the odd bit of playing. I'd love to play for ballet classes again; now that really is fun," she enthused.

"That's a good idea," agreed Steve, "but you'd have to think it through carefully before you give up your job. Mind you," he continued, putting his arm round Lucy for a few moments, "I'm sure a girl of your talents could pick up any amount of work. I bet you're really brilliant!"

"I don't know about that," laughed Lucy. "I don't seem to have had time to play anything serious for ages. Of course, I really miss having a piano to practise on in the evenings. Angela, our next door neighbour, has said I can use their piano any time I want to, but I don't like to be a nuisance and to be honest, I'm so shattered by the time I've marked my books and sorted out what I'm teaching the next day that I usually just end up half asleep on the sofa watching some rubbish on the telly in the evenings."

"I know the feeling," sympathised Steve.

"But I don't know why you're letting me moan on like this," continued Lucy. "You're looking after your parents too, on top of all your school work, aren't you? How are things going?"

"Actually, much better than I had anticipated," replied Steve. "Mum's tired but basically on the mend. It's Dad that needs the help now; it's all been such a strain on him. But they certainly don't need me around all the time now, otherwise I wouldn't have been free this weekend, I suppose."

Lucy nodded sympathetically.

"Look," said Steve hesitantly. "What would you think, would you like, I mean we're very near my parents' cottage, only ten minutes in the car. I could give them a ring and, that is, if you'd like, we could drop in on them for a cup of tea."

Steve had had this plan at the back of his mind ever since he phoned Lucy that morning, but wasn't sure whether she would want to meet his parents or whether he'd have the courage to suggest it.

"Steve!" said Lucy. "What a wonderful idea!"

Steve smiled in relief, made the phone call and they were soon on their way to Bakesville.

"Steve! How lovely to see you. And Lucy too! We've heard so much about you," said Steve's father, David, as he greeted them at the door of his cottage.

Lucy looked at Steve in astonishment. She had no idea that Steve would have mentioned her to his parents. She appreciated how friendly Steve had been to her but she knew he couldn't be keen on her except as a friend; why, he knew how silly she had been over Tristan. He knew exactly the sort of little fool she was.

"Oh, hello, it's lovely to meet you," Lucy said to Steve's father. Suddenly she realised that she cared very much what Steve thought of her; she realised that she cared for Steve; she realised that…Oh, thought Lucy. I feel so confused. She nearly tripped as they went into the cottage and Steve put out a hand to steady her.

"Careful," he cautioned. "These flagstones may be picturesque, but they're a death trap for the unwary."

Lucy felt a blush sweep over her from her toes to the top of her head. I love him, she thought. I really love him and I've completely blown it. He must think I'm pathetic.

"Let's have a cup of tea," suggested Steve's father.

"Where's Mum?" asked Steve. "Is she OK?"

"She's having a little rest, lying down upstairs. Nothing to worry about; she's just tired. I've left the baby monitor on, so that she can call down to us."

"The baby monitor?" asked Lucy in astonishment. Steve and his father both laughed at Lucy's puzzled expression.

"When Mum was really ill," explained Steve, "we borrowed my sister Charlotte's baby monitor that she had used when her kids were tiny. She didn't need it any more and I thought it might be useful for Mum. Dad wanted to sit with her all the time, but with the monitor on, he could nip downstairs and make a pot of tea or whatever and she could call for him if necessary without having to raise her voice and he could hear her breathing to reassure him when he wasn't in the bedroom."

"I see," said Lucy smiling. "What a great idea!"

"Steve," called a faint crackly voice form the baby monitor. "Is that my Steve?"

"Your mother must have heard you come in," said Steve's father. "Why don't you go up, Steve and help your mother down the stairs. I know she'd like to meet Lucy."

"And I'd like to meet her too," said Lucy. "Can I help you with the tea?" she continued, turning to Steve's father.

"That's kind of you, Lucy," said David. "There's really no need, though. You wait here, Lucy. I'll be back in a minute."

"And so will I," said Steve, disappearing upstairs. "Make yourself at home, Lucy. Try the piano if you want; it's just over there."

"Oh," cried Lucy in delight. "I'd love to try it. Thank you!"

She sat down at the piano, an old Bechstein upright and tried a few chords. It's got a lovely sweet, rich sound, but it could do with tuning, thought Lucy critically. She started playing a Chopin waltz, then paused, hearing the crackly sound again. That must be the baby monitor, she thought. They haven't turned it off.

"I'm so pleased that Emma's having a baby," said Steve's mum.

"Well, so am I really," said Steve, "but I hope she can cope. It's a big responsibility."

"Of course she can cope," said Steve's mum. "I know how much you worry about Emma."

"Emma means so much to me," said Steve seriously. "I want everything to go well for her."

I shouldn't be listening to this, thought Lucy, suddenly embarrassed and she resumed playing her Chopin waltz and was soon lost in the music again. When the waltz drew to its conclusion, she sat back in satisfaction and then became aware of the conversation upstairs again.

"And what do you think she feels?" asked Steve's mum.

Oh, thought Lucy. They're still talking about the mysterious Emma, the mysterious and pregnant Emma.

Lucy's hands ran idly up and down the keyboard,

picking out chords.

"I really love her," said Steve passionately.

Lucy's hands paused on a minor chord and she took her foot off the pedal.

"I want to marry her but I don't think she's sure of herself at the moment. That makes things more complicated, you know, with all that has happened. She said herself that she'd been a bit foolish."

"You can't blame all that on her," said Steve's mother gently. "It takes two people to be foolish, you know, and she's very young."

Lucy gasped in horror. Steve loved this Emma and wanted to marry her. They had both been "foolish" and now she was having a baby.

Lucy began playing a sad, simple Nocturne. She knew now that Steve didn't want her; he had only been showing her friendship and concern. But wait a minute, she thought angrily. Steve was showing her a bit too much concern. She remembered his hand round her shoulders during their walk today and the kiss on her cheek when he had come round to her flat this morning. Lucy started to play Chopin's "Funeral March." Steve was trying to chat her up while he was involved with the wretched Emma. He was no better than that rat, Tristan, he was…

"Please don't stop playing," begged David, appearing suddenly at Lucy's elbow as she slammed the lid of the piano shut. "Don't you like our piano? I know it's quite old and a little bit neglected; we keep meaning to give the piano tuner a ring, but what with one thing and another, we haven't got round to it."

"Oh," said Lucy, mortified. "It's not that, it's just, oh, how rude of me, the lid must have slipped, I mean…"

"Have a cup of tea," offered David. "Here come the other two. Good! Let's all sit down."

"Lucy! How lovely to meet you," said Steve's mother.

What a very sad expression she has, thought Steve's mother. This business with the conductor really has knocked her for six. Poor lamb. Still, I can quite see why my Steve's so much in love with her. She's a stunning girl.

Lucy did not say much during tea, nor during the drive back to Springfield. I expect she's brooding about Tristan, thought Steve. I won't bother to chat to him, thought Lucy angrily as they sped towards Stanhope Gardens. He doesn't deserve it. I won't be made a fool of again by a man. I shall die an old maid. See if I care!

"Thank you for the lift," she said stiffly as she climbed out of the car.

"See you soon," called Steve, "at choir on Wednesday."

"See you sometime," replied Lucy.

She couldn't be bothered to tell him that she wouldn't be at choir on Wednesday, as it was her school concert. Under different circumstances, she might have asked him to come to it, but now she knew the truth, she wouldn't make a fool of herself again by running after a man who was involved with someone else.

Thus it was that on Wednesday evening, Steve wondered anxiously where Lucy was when she didn't appear at choir. I hope she's not ill, he thought. It would take a lot to make her miss choir. Tristan too wondered where Lucy was, as he felt vaguely that he owed her some sort of apology. But I never apologise, he remembered, tossing his few remaining curls as he conducted. I'm always right and this concert is going to be magnificent, simply magnificent.

During the interval, Steve approached Deborah, Lucy's section leader, who was chatting to Angela and Sarah.

"Deborah," he began. "I don't suppose you know where Lucy is this evening?"

"Lucy?" said Deborah. "Well, she excused herself from the rehearsal, but I don't know where she is."

"I know," said Sarah. "It's Lucy's school concert this

evening. That's where she is."

"Yes," added Angela. "I saw her going out at about six o'clock, all dressed up; very excited she was, looking forward to the performance."

"Oh," said Steve, rather subdued. "I thought she would have told me about it. I mean, she did tell me about it, but I didn't realise it was tonight. I would have liked to have gone."

"Oh dear," said Sarah sympathetically. "I'm sure Lucy didn't mean to offend you. Perhaps she thought you wouldn't be interested?"

"Or perhaps she thought it wasn't good enough?" ventured Angela.

"Or perhaps she didn't give a toss," snarled Steve angrily as he turned his back on the three women and stormed back to his seat.

It was all falling into place now, he thought. Lucy was rather cold and odd after we had visited my parents on Sunday. Steve remembered the long silence in the car as they had driven back to Springfield. I put that down to tiredness on Lucy's part, thought Steve angrily, but now I see that she simply couldn't be bothered. She was just using me to get over Tristan.

She doesn't care for me at all and I suppose there's no reason why she should either, continued Steve bitterly. I'm not much of a catch. Just a boring old school teacher, not glamorous enough for someone like Lucy, I suppose. Steve sighed heavily.

"You all right?" asked his neighbour in the basses.

"Never better," lied Steve and soon they were working their way through the last chorus.

"For great Babylon's fallen…" sang Steve, his voice cracking on the high notes and his eyes swimming with tears.

Chapter Twelve: Praise ye the Gods!

"Get into the car! Now!" Caroline's voice echoed up the stairs as she called to the children. "Come on! If we don't go soon, we'll miss Lucy's rehearsal."

It was Saturday afternoon and Springfield Choral Society was rehearsing with the orchestra in preparation for the concert in the evening. Caroline and her family were staying up in London with Sarah and Jeremy. Caroline was taking her twins and Sarah's son James to part of the rehearsal, so that they could see Lucy and Sarah singing. It was felt, at least by the adults, that the children were too young to stay up for the actual concert, so Lucy had suggested they came to part of the rehearsal to listen.

"It's will be fairly chaotic," she had explained, "and no one will mind a few people listening, in fact in a way it helps us to have an audience."

Eventually Caroline rounded up the children, strapped them safely into the car and they were on their way.

"Quieten down!" Caroline yelled as they sped towards the church where the rehearsal and later the concert were to be held.

"Quieten down and stop squabbling! Do you want to see Lucy and Sarah singing or not?"

"Of course we do Mummy," chanted Rebecca and Teresa in unison.

"I'm so glad Thomas isn't here," said James smugly.

"James! That's not very nice," said Caroline. "Why do you want to be so nasty about your little brother? You know the only reason he's not coming is because he's too young."

James smirked at Caroline in the mirror.

"And," warned Caroline, "it's not too late for me to take you home to your Dad and leave you there."

James hung his head in shame.

"Sorry," he sobbed. "Actually, I wish Thomas was here. I miss him."

Rebecca and Teresa rolled their eyes at each other but said nothing.

"Here's the church," said Caroline. "I'll find a space in the car park. No, girls, don't undo your seat belts until I've stopped. You know that's the rule."

As Caroline swung into the car park, she narrowly avoided hitting Angela, who was scurrying into the rehearsal, bag and coat flying, at least twenty minutes late.

"Sorry!" Caroline called out of the window. "Desperately sorry! OK?"

Angela turned and nodded, then ran into the church. She managed to scramble up to her seat in the sopranos without Tristan noticing how late she was.

"Thanks for saving me a seat," she breathed to Lucy. "I just couldn't get away in time. Amy was being rather difficult, you know."

"Don't worry," smiled Lucy. "I told Deborah you'd been unavoidably detained and anyway, you're not the only one late. Look at them!"

Angela looked down the aisle of the church and saw several basses, among them Steve, creeping up to the platform as unobtrusively as they could.

"Good evening gentlemen," said Tristan sarcastically as he spun round and noticed them. "When you're ready…"

At least all the orchestra is here, thought Tristan with a frown. He was desperate to get properly started with the rehearsal. I can't relax until I've heard the balance between the choir and the orchestra, he fretted. God, I wish I'd brought my hip flask of whisky. I usually bring it to rehearsals, but it seems to have disappeared since Claire's been around.

"Ladies and gentlemen," Tristan bellowed. "From the top! And could the choir please remember that there is an orchestra here today. You have to project your voices!"

The choir certainly hadn't forgotten that there was an orchestra there. The orchestral players had been objects of intense scrutiny since the beginning of the rehearsal, particularly the very young and handsome cellist sitting under Tristan's right hand.

"He's gorgeous," murmured one of the more impressionable women and some of the tenors looked interested too. "Is he wearing a wedding ring?"

"Concentrate!" bellowed Tristan.

At this moment, Caroline sneaked into the back row of seats with the three children.

"Shhh!" she cautioned. "Let's see if we can see Lucy and Sarah."

"Mummy!" yelled James. "There! That's my Mummy!"

Tristan glared angrily at the back of the church, while Caroline put her head down behind a pew.

Muffled laughter broke out in the choir. Steve looked across at Lucy and saw that she wasn't laughing or even smiling. She looks exhausted, he thought. Completely washed out. Lucy looked in Steve's direction and then away immediately as she noticed that he was looking at her.

"The rat!" she moaned under her breath. "How dare he look at me!"

Soon the rehearsal was underway again.

"Blow the trumpet in the new moon," sang the choir while Rebecca, Teresa and James gazed up at the performers in awe.

"It's so loud," Rebecca whispered to Teresa.

"It hurts my ears," Teresa whispered back.

Caroline shot a warning look in their direction.

The balance is wrong, thought Tristan on the podium. Why can't the band accompany properly? Why do they have to drown the singers? I hope it will be all right; better do the last big number next..."

"Break," said the leader of the orchestra, waving his violin in the air to get everyone's attention "Break! It's our break time. We've been playing for long enough."

Tristan agreed meekly to this demand, much to the

astonishment of the choir.

"Well, they are professionals," Deborah explained to the sopranos sitting around her. "They need regular breaks, otherwise they get too tired. It's all in their union rules. Anyway, don't forget there are two other pieces in this concert that we're not in, a Mozart overture and a Vivaldi Concerto. The orchestra have been hard at work rehearsing those pieces before we even got here."

Lucy took advantage of the break to go to the back of the church and see her sister and the children.

"What did you think?" she asked James. "Oh look! Here's Sarah - here's your Mummy coming to see you as well."

"It's too loud, Mummy," said James seriously. "We all think so."

"Just wait until you hear the end," laughed Sarah. "Then you'll know what loud means!"

"I'll see you again this evening, Lucy," said Caroline. "I think I'll take the kids back soon. They've probably had enough. Oh and I forgot to tell you that Mum's coming this evening too."

"What!" cried Lucy in astonishment. "Mum? Isn't she in France? What is she doing over here? She isn't due until nearer Christmas."

"She managed to get an earlier flight and she's already been in London for a couple of days, rushing round the art galleries and shops, you know how she is and staying with her old friend Sally," explained Caroline. "So she'll come to the concert tonight because she's dying to see you then she'll stay at Sarah's for the night with the rest of us and come back to Bath tomorrow with us."

"Great," said Lucy. "I'm so pleased but I wish she'd let me know she was in London already so that I could have seen her sooner. Oh, how exciting! I can't wait!"

"And you will be seeing much more of her," said Caroline mysteriously. "But I'll tell you more later. You'd better get back now. They're calling the choir to their seats."

As Lucy went back to her place, she had to walk past Steve.

"Lucy!" he said urgently. "Lucy! Please can we talk? Why didn't you tell me about your concert on Wednesday? What's wrong?"

"I know what's going on, Steve," hissed Lucy angrily. "I won't be two timed again, not after Tristan. How could you? Oh, I don't even want to talk to you."

With that, Lucy rushed back to her seat, leaving Steve open mouthed with astonishment. What on earth is she talking about, he wondered. Two timing? I've no idea what she means.

During the second half of the rehearsal Steve puzzled and puzzled over Lucy's remarks and behaviour. He tried to pinpoint exactly when Lucy had started to act in a peculiar way and by the end of the rehearsal he had worked out that it was at his parents' house when he had gone up to see his mother. Is she jealous of my mother, Steve wondered. Surely not. Or did Dad say something to put her off? Perhaps he told her about my old girlfriends, but no; it's more than that. I give up. Women! Still, I'll have a word with Dad, in case there's some confusion. It just doesn't make sense.

"Watch the beat, basses!" yelled Tristan. "Sing up, sopranos!"

Tristan winked at Claire as he looked at her row and she smirked back. She spent most of her time at Tristan's house now and had decided to move in with him formally in the New Year. She would tell him her plans at Christmas, when the moment was right.

Lucy was fuming at Steve's cheek in approaching her during the rehearsal. How dare he ask her about her school concert? Of course she wouldn't have asked him to come to it, after his betrayal. Lucy looked steadily at Tristan as he conducted and she counted the lines on his face. And he's got a beer belly too, she thought in distaste. Claire's welcome to him. She can have Steve as well if he decides he needs another woman apart from the mysterious Emma.

"Are you all right, Lucy?" asked Angela anxiously. "It's just that you've missed two entries and I only get the note because you sing it first and so I'm lost now."

"Oh sorry," apologised Lucy. "I'm a bit upset; tell you about it later."

Lucy noticed Caroline and the children sneaking out of the rehearsal. She was very glad they had had the chance to hear some of it. Caroline and Jeremy, together with Brian, Sarah's husband, would all be in the audience tonight and a baby sitter would be looking after the four children. She'll have her hands full, thought Lucy with a grin. They should pay her double rate. Lucy was longing to see her mother. I'll tell her about Steve, she thought, but perhaps not about Tristan.

After the rehearsal, Lucy went home by bus with Angela.

"Is Jeffrey coming to the concert this evening?" Lucy asked Angela. "Have you got a babysitter for little Amy?"

"I booked a babysitter ages ago; there's no way I'd let Jeffrey miss my debut with the choir," grinned Angela. "But what about you; what's upset you, Lucy? You said you'd tell me later and it's later now but of course if you'd rather not say anything, I'll understand."

Lucy told Angela everything and then Angela was as puzzled as Lucy was upset.

"Are you sure you've got this right, Lucy?" Angela demanded. "After all, you might have misheard the conversation and it doesn't really seem possible that Steve would behave that badly. Why, he seems such a nice young man. He even reminds me of my Jeffrey when I first met him."

"The baby monitor was very clear," said Lucy sadly. "I wish I could be wrong about it, truly I do, but I know I can't trust anyone now after Tristan and then Steve too.

I'm just hopeless, aren't I? I always pick the wrong ones."

"This doesn't seem right to me," said Angela, very worried now. "Would you like me to talk to Steve?"

"Oh no," replied Lucy, absolutely horrified. "Please don't! Oh look; here's our stop. How long have we got before the concert?"

"Just long enough to eat and get changed," said Angela frowning. "But probably not long enough to sort Amy out. I must dash! Shall we go to the concert together?"

"Well actually I'm meeting Caroline and the rest of my family for a quick drink before the concert," said Lucy. "You're more than welcome to come along too."

"Better not," replied Angela. "I'll have to read Amy her bedtime story and settle her or she'll never let me out this evening! See you tonight, Lucy and thanks so much for saving me a place!"

"See you," called Lucy as she let herself into the flat.

Julia was there, getting ready to go out.

"Where to this evening?" teased Lucy. "How many times have you been out with Mark since you met him last Saturday at Grangewood Golf Club?"

"Only three times," smiled Julia. "Anyway, tonight we're both coming to your concert."

"But you don't like music," said Lucy in astonishment. "At least not this sort of music."

"No, but I want to see you and Mark wants to support Steve and I'm sure we'll enjoy it. How is Steve, anyway? Have you sorted things out yet?"

"There is no Steve," answered Lucy stiffly. "He tried to talk to me today but I'm not interested and no thanks, I don't want to talk about it. I'm off to have a shower and get ready."

"Well I think it's a shame," Julia called after her. "And I still don't understand why you're being so mean to him."

Julia shook her head, very puzzled over Lucy's behaviour. Lucy had not told anyone at all about what she had overheard on the baby monitor, anyone that is, except Angela today. She had felt too embarrassed to burden Julia with all her problems, especially after Tristan and anyway, Lucy and Julia had hardly seen each other all week.

"It's very puzzling," said Julia aloud and she resolved to ask Mark about it, to see if he knew what was going on. Julia glanced up at the mantelpiece and looked at the picture of Lucy there, drawn by Robert Nibbet. Oh Lucy, thought Julia. Your love life is never uncomplicated, is it?

Most of the choir seemed to be crammed into the pub before the concert, the men in their dinner jackets and the ladies in their long black dresses.

"Now don't forget," Deborah was instructing a group of altos. "You must sit on the platform in your places for the first half of the concert, even though you're not singing in the Mozart or the Vivaldi.

"And try to look interested, sweeties," drawled Tristan as he walked past the singers, butting in on Deborah's lecture. "The last thing the orchestra wants is a bunch of women chatting behind them, especially in the Vivaldi, which has some very tricky bits."

Tristan fingered his collar nervously. He was desperate for a drink to steady his nerves, but Claire had absolutely forbidden it and he was beginning to feel a little scared of her. He settled for a quick cigarette in the corner of the pub, puffing deeply as if his life depended on it. Who is that elegant woman over there, he wondered. She's a bit of all right, for an older bird that is. Reminds me of someone: can't think who. Christ, I'd better get back to the church and check my music is in place.

Lucy's mother noticed Tristan looking at her and turned to her daughter.

"Is that Tristan, your conductor, Lucy? He looks terribly nervous. Very highly strung, I should think."

"Yes," hissed Lucy with a frown. "That's Tristan."

Oh dear, thought Caroline. I never did have that sisterly little chat with Lucy about Tristan, still, now Mum's back, I can hand it over to her and she can sort it all out.

"What's this big surprise you were talking about, Caroline?" asked Lucy.

"Darling Lucy," began her mother. "After all these years, I'm going to move back to Bath."

"What!" cried Lucy. "Oh Mum, I'm so pleased! When? I mean, have you sold the flat in France?"

"Not yet," smiled Lucy's Mum. "I'll go back in the New Year to sort things out and then move back for good. I'll have my work cut out sorting out the house in Bath, I can tell you, after the last lot of tenants, but I'll enjoy it too. In fact, I can't wait to get started."

"Mum," said Lucy, hugging her mother, with tears springing into her eyes. "Mum! You don't know how much I've missed you for the last few years. I was so afraid you'd settle in France for good. You thought that too, didn't you, Caroline?"

"It did cross my mind once or twice," admitted Caroline, "but I still thought Mum would come home in the end. And true to form, Mum has already found herself an admirer. Got chatting at an art gallery, didn't you Mum and ended up going out for a drink."

"Well, yes," smiled Lucy's mum. "Bob is rather a sweetie, a real gentleman, why he even said he would try to come to the concert tonight. He can only make the second half, but really wants to meet my two girls. Perhaps we can all go for a drink afterwards?"

"Golly!" said Lucy in admiration. "Fast work Mum!"

Lucy's mother acknowledged the compliment by patting her elegant head of hair delicately. She had been a redhead in her youth, like Lucy, but her hair was now blonde and silver and twisted into a simple chignon, secured with a tortoiseshell clasp.

"I've got a surprise for you too, Mum," said Lucy. "I've more or less decided to give up class teaching. Don't worry, I'll stick the year out, but I'd like to build up some freelance teaching and playing and then be self employed from September."

"That's nice dear," said Lucy's mother vaguely. "I didn't know you weren't happy in that school of yours. You never said."

"I think it's the right decision," said Lucy firmly. "Anyway, plenty of time to decide."

Steve watched Lucy and her family from the other end of the pub, not knowing whether he wanted to turn his back on her or rush up to her and cover her in kisses.

The pub door swung open at that point and Steve's parents, his twin sister and brothers in law came in. Lucy noticed at once that Emma was wearing a smock shaped garment and looked positively glowing. Lucy turned away, fighting back the tears.

"Time ladies and gentlemen of the choir, please," boomed Deborah. "Time to take your seats!"

The noise level in the pub rose as with a flurry of black skirts and excited giggles, the ladies of the choir made a dash for the door to make their way to the church over the road where the concert was to be held.

"You too gentlemen," intoned one of the basses, supposedly in charge of the bass section. "You heard the lady. No, there isn't time for another drink! Off you go!"

The traffic outside was at a complete standstill as the singers flocked across the road, clasping their black choir folders.

"Someone's left their music behind," shouted a tenor.

"Oops! Thanks!"

"Hey! Mind out! You're treading on my hem."

"I can't wait to see that gorgeous young violin soloist again, can you?"

"Isn't he sensational? Where does he come from?"

"Russia, I think. He looks Russian, anyway."

"He's probably from Staines. You can't tell by looks, you know."

"Quick! We need to line up. It's time for the back row to go on."

The choir had to squeeze onto the platform in their rows before the orchestra filed on. As usual, several choir members got out of order and had to push past lines of singers already in their places to reach their destination.

"Hey! Budge up can't you? I haven't got enough room here."

"We haven't got enough room because Deborah's in our row."

"Well, it was OK in the rehearsal."

"Anyone got a throat sweet? No? Can you pass the message on?"

Throat sweets and tissues were being busily passed up and down the rows of sopranos and altos while the men chatted noisily and tried to find places to put their feet.

"Awfully narrow these steps, aren't they? Can't see how we'll be comfortable for the concert."

Lucy was one of the last sopranos to take her place as she was sitting in the front row. Just as she was filing up to the platform, she saw Julia, sitting with Mark. They had seats near the front of the church, next to the aisle. Julia took the chance to dash out and whisper urgently to Lucy.

"Oh Lucy, do forgive Steve, whatever he's done. He's looking so forlorn. I saw him gazing at you as you came in. He's got all his family in the audience with him you know; they're in the audience just behind us and one of his sisters is expecting. Oh Luce, good luck! See you later."

Startled, Lucy turned to look at the audience.

"Oh Lucy, hurry up! We've got to get onto the platform. The orchestra are waiting," whispered Sarah who was right behind Lucy in the line.

"Sorry," said Lucy, her heart pounding. She hadn't quite taken in what Julia had said yet. She stumbled to her place in the choir and sat down heavily. Looking over the rows of faces, she recognised Steve's parents and they seemed to be smiling at her. Next to them sat two women. Twins, thought Lucy, of course, Steve's twin sisters. I remember now, but I don't understand. Lucy frowned as she tried to work out what was going on. How could I have been mistaken, she thought. What was I doing when I heard about Emma? Oh dear, she thought and began to tremble. I was playing the piano. Perhaps I missed some of the conversation, perhaps I made a mistake? But who was Steve talking about then? Who is it that he's in love with? Oh, perhaps it's me? Perhaps… Lucy put her hands up to her face in shame and confusion. And now I've ruined it all over again, she thought in an agony of embarrassment. I've been so cold towards him, so horrible; he'll never forgive me for this and I don't blame him. Lucy could not bring herself to look across at Steve and the Mozart overture and the Vivaldi Concerto passed in a blur for her. She made her way outside as soon as the interval started, desperate for some fresh air as she felt so light headed.

"Where's that young lady of yours got to, Steve?" asked Steve's father in the interval. "Where's Lucy?"

"I don't know," answered Steve miserably. "And I don't know what's wrong with her, either. She hasn't been acting normally for ages now, ever since she met you and Mum, actually. No Dad; it's not a joke! Suddenly she can't seem to stand me, you know and I thought I was really getting somewhere. Did you say anything to her, while I was upstairs with Mum, you know, to put her off? She seems to have some crazy idea that I'm involved with someone else."

"I hardly said a word to her," said Steve's father in astonishment. "Most of the time she was playing the piano, that's what I could hear, oh and I could hear that annoying baby monitor too. We could hear you talking upstairs. Why didn't you switch the monitor off, Steve? It gets on my nerves sometimes and you never know, someone might overhear something they're not meant to one day."

"Yes," gasped Steve, comprehension dawning. "I suppose they might. Excuse me Dad. I've got to find Lucy really quickly!"

Steve pushed through the crowds at the back of the church with uncharacteristic force.

"Sarah! Deborah! Do you know where Lucy is?"

"Outside I think," said Sarah. "She rushed out as soon as the interval started. I hope she's all right."

"Thanks," shouted Steve as he made a dash for the door. He saw Lucy immediately, leaning against the church wall, gazing up at the moon. She must have realised the truth by now, he thought.

"Lucy," Steve said. "Lucy; come here. Oh my darling," he murmured as he took her in his arms. "I've just got one word to say to you, or perhaps it's two, not sure, anyway, it's baby monitor!"

"You know!" whispered Lucy. "Oh, I'm so embarrassed. I've been so horrible to you! Oh, why are you laughing? It's not funny!"

"Yes it is," insisted Steve. "You know it is; it's ridiculous. Why, how could you even think such a thing of me? Oh Lucy, I do love you!"

"You're not angry then?" asked Lucy, still unsure.

"What do you think?" asked Steve as he bent his head to kiss her.

"Any choir out here? Time to go back," boomed Deborah's voice. "Come on you two; hurry up!"

Steve and Lucy hurried inside, holding hands and giggling. Tristan moved out of the shadows where he had been enjoying a quick cigarette to calm his nerves. "Very curious," he remarked to the empty air. "Strange how things work out."

Lucy's sister Caroline was sitting in the audience with her mother and her husband Jeremy, hoping that "Belshazzar," or whatever it was, wouldn't be too long. She was anxious to get back to Rebecca and Teresa to make sure they were all right because they weren't always happy to be left with a baby sitter. She stared in amazement as Lucy ran into the church holding hands with a very attractive and suitable looking young man and then felt very relieved as she realised she wouldn't have to talk to her mother about Lucy's obsession with Tristan. One thing off my list to worry about, she thought gratefully. Now I can start thinking about Christmas dinner. I wonder how many sprouts I will need? Maybe more now if Lucy's young man joins us and I think I know where I can buy some still on the stalk, organic of course and there's that new recipe where you stir fry them with chestnuts…

The choir were soon safely installed in their places and the orchestra filed on and began the long process of tuning up.

"Just look at that lady playing the oboe," whispered Jeremy to Caroline "Her mouth is all screwed up. Is that right?"

"Let's not allow our girls to play the oboe," Caroline answered. "They'd look much nicer playing the flute, wouldn't they?"

Lucy could see Mary Goodshoe in the second row with her two sons Michael and Cuthbert. She nearly waved at them but managed to restrain herself. I'm no better than the children, she thought to herself with a giggle.

"Look Angela," Lucy said. "There's your Jeffrey trying to catch your eye. Can you see him?"

"Where? I can't see him!"

"I think Brian has finally noticed where I'm sitting," whispered Sarah from the row behind Lucy.

"Yes! Yes! I can see Jeffrey. Oh, I do hope he'll enjoy the concert."

"Bound to. Look! Here comes Tristan!"

As Tristan advanced towards the platform, resplendent in his tailcoat, one of the basses remarked unkindly,

"Old Tristan's had his hair blow dried for the concert!"

A ripple of coarse laughter ran through the bass section, soon masked by the applause from the audience for Tristan's entrance.

"Isn't he splendid," whispered Claire to herself. "And he's all mine!"

"Thus spake Isaiah," intoned the tenors and basses.

"Thy sons that thou shalt beget,

They shall be taken away and be eunuchs…"

Robert Nibbet was enjoying the music from his seat near the back of the church. He had managed to get there just after the beginning of the second half and had already spotted where Lucy's mother was sitting. He was very smitten with her.

"Didn't expect it at my time of life, I must say," he exclaimed to himself in amazement. "She really is perfect."

He suddenly noticed Lucy in the front row of the sopranos, singing her heart out. Why, it's the girl from the train, thought Robert in astonishment and she looks like, why of course, her mother! How wonderful! And she looks so bright and happy today, not at all like before. Well, well, what a magical evening. And with that, he settled back contentedly in his seat.

The piece seemed to flash past in minutes for the choir. All their weeks of preparation and hard work were paying off and even Tristan began to look pleased. Lucy caught Tristan's eye at one point and then hurriedly looked away.

"Thou art weighed in the balance and found wanting," chanted the tenors and basses.

Claire smirked at Tristan. She knew she had him where she wanted now.

"Slain!" shouted the choir.

On and on went the music, like some gigantic unstoppable machine. The brass players were red in the face, veins standing out on their necks most unhealthily.

"Weep, Wail," sang the choir.

No more of that for me, thought Lucy joyfully, her voice cracking with emotion on the top notes. All will be well now.

In the front row, Miss Greymitt was thoroughly enjoying the music and was proud to have been part of its preparation. Although I know it was such an insignificant part, she thought to herself as her brown lace up shoe tapped the pulse of the music gently on the stone floor of the church.

"Make a joyful noise to the God of Jacob…

Alleluia, alleluia."

Tristan controlled the orchestra magnificently as the choir sang their last "Alleluia," and then let the players go full throttle to the piece's triumphant conclusion.

A stunned pause followed as the audience allowed the last chord to echo through the church, bouncing off pillars, walls and floor. Lucy and Steve looked at each other with love in their hearts and tenderness in their faces.

Then the audience roared and shouted, many jumping to their feet.

"Bravo!"

"Magnificent!"

"Who would have thought to hear this in Springfield?"

"Well, Tristan hasn't lost his touch, that's for sure!"

"Thank you, thank you," murmured Tristan as he took bow after bow. When he finally acknowledged the choir, the audience clapped even louder. Tristan looked surprised but quickly changed his expression to one of pride and dignity.

"Bravo choir!"

"Encore, encore!"

Epilogue:
In one hour is her judgement come

On a bright Saturday in July the following year, Lucy and Steve were married in a pretty little church in Bath, with all their friends and family watching.

"Steve," whispered Lucy as they came down the aisle. "Steve! I can't believe this is really happening!"

"Oh, I do love you, Lucy," Steve sighed. He pulled Lucy closer to him as they walked out of the church into the sparkling sunshine to begin their lives together.

On the same day, Claire and Tristan were married in Springfield Registry Office.

"Tristan," whispered Claire as they posed for photographs on the steps. "Tristan! I can't believe this is really happening! Just think! We'll be a real family in time for Christmas this year."

Tristan looked at the very large bouquet Claire was holding over her bump, then turned away and plucked at his collar.

"Slain!" he muttered bitterly to himself. "Slain!"

ABOUT THE AUTHOR

Jenny Worstall spent her childhood years in Devon, Bath, Dorset and Naples. She is a musician and teacher and has sung in many choirs and choral societies, including the BBC Symphony Chorus, where she met her husband. Jenny now lives in London with her husband and two children.

Make a Joyful Noise is her first novel.

Visit her website for further information:

www.jennyworstall.webspace.virginmedia.com

2714621R00110

Printed in Great Britain
by Amazon.co.uk, Ltd.,
Marston Gate.